Christmas Magic
Magic
At Holly Oaks

RACQUEL HENRY

RACQUEL HENRY BOOKS

Published by Racquel Henry Books, a division of Henry Co., LLC

First Edition.

For more about Racquel and her books, please visit her website: www.racquelhenry.com.

ISBN (trade paperback): 978-1-959787-06-8
ISBN (ebook): 978-1-959787-07-5

Cover design by Natalie Henry-Charles at Pretty Peacock Paperie
Developmental Editing by Nicole McCurdy at Emerald Edits
Proofreading by Jenn Lockwood Editing
Interior design by Book Obsessed Formatting

*For The Unit always: Mommy, Daddy, Nat Nat, Jeffy, Ella,
Roman, and Titan*

But especially, my sister, my ride-or-die, Natalie.

Content Details

Though it's fairly light, *Christmas Magic at Holly Oaks* does include grief and the mention of the death of a parent.

Also By Racquel Henry:

Holiday on Park
Letter to Santa
Christmas in Cardwick
Meet Me in December

One

The loud sound of an engine cutting through clouds. Stagnant cold air. A child screaming their own rendition of "Jingle Bells" on repeat a few rows back. A captain with a voice as jolly as Santa Claus and a beard to match. All of them work to grate my last nerve. I keep my jaw clenched and wonder if all the tension building there just might crack my teeth. I'm still trying to figure out how I let Sharlene talk me into getting on this plane headed to a town that treats Christmas like it's a beauty pageant when I, in fact, hate Christmas. Not only is it too early in the morning for this, but I should be back home, emailing potential clients. But here I am, at 35,000 feet altitude, because my sister thinks I need a change of pace. According to Sharlene, spending Christmas where there's snow will be fun.

Sharlene places a hand on my arm. "We're going to have a good trip, Rose. Promise."

I roll my eyes. "But I had plans to sulk around my apartment and eat Kiss Cakes all season."

Sharlene squeezes my arm. "Now what good would that do?"

I shoot her an annoyed look.

"So we didn't land the client. You know Gran would say—"

"Everything happens for a reason," I finish. "Yeah, yeah, I know." I love my sister, and respect her optimism, but securing Fern Gardens would have been life changing for our business. They're one of the most successful botanical gardens in Orlando. People travel from around the world just to visit it. And securing a contract with them would have meant consistent work for the next five years.

Sharlene smiles. "She was always right. This just means we'll find something better. And now you can enjoy the holiday season without all the jitters that come from trying to impress a new client."

I roll my eyes once again. "You know I couldn't care less about the holiday season. I hate this time of year."

Sharlene lets out a dramatic sigh. "Yes, we know, oh Queen of the Christmas Curmudgeons. But I *love* Christmas. And can you give this a chance? We've never seen snow, and now we get to spend ten days together in the middle of a town that might as well be the Christmas capital of the US. We haven't had a sisters' trip in forever."

Can't argue with her on that, and while I hate Christmas with the passion of a thousand sparkly bulbs, I adore my sister. We've both been so focused on living the plant life to grow our company, that it hasn't left much time for trips. Up until about four years ago, we'd take multiple sister trips each year. Neither of us had our own significant others or families, so it had been easy to get away. But our co-owned business, Plant Ladies, took off, and with that level of success came the cost of travel time.

I let out a deep breath. "I'm here, aren't I?"

Sharlene smiles. "Yeah, but you've been sulking since we arrived at the airport." She folds her arms over her chest.

"Fine, I'll try a little harder," I grumble. I mean it too, though I know it will be difficult. As much as this isn't my holiday jam—too many sad memories always want to rise to the surface for me—I don't want to ruin the trip for Sharlene. She doesn't have to know that internally I'm screaming and smashing Christmas lightbulbs.

Two

I almost trip as we step off the plane and onto the airplane jet bridge. It adds more salt on my mood. "I can't believe I let you talk me into this."

"Will you chill? This is supposed to be a vacation. We've literally been here three seconds, and you're already curmudgeon complaining." Sharlene glances up at the screen in front of us. "We're carousel two. It's this way." She points to the left then heads in that direction.

I follow, but I drag my feet. "I should be at home in my pajamas, with a nice cup of tea, researching more potential clients."

Sharlene smirks at me over her shoulder. "You can do that here—but make those pajamas Christmas. I got

4

us matching pairs."

I groan. "What am I supposed to do with them after Christmas?" Seasonal clothes are a mystery. Why would I buy something that I can only wear a few times a year?

"You can still wear them whenever you want—like I do. I promise the Christmas Fashion Police will not show up at your door."

Her answer doesn't surprise me at all. She's the person posting a countdown to Christmas the day after Christmas. "You know how I feel about wasting money on stuff like that."

"That's exactly why I bought them. And come on, Rose. It's. Fun." She shakes her head.

We wait for about fifteen minutes, grab our bags off the carousel, then head outside. Sharlene stops mid-step and gasps.

I run into her back. "Really?"

She gestures to our surroundings. "Look at all this! Can't tell me this isn't the most magical thing you've ever seen."

In the distance are snow-covered mountains against the backdrop of a surprisingly cerulean sky. There are more Christmas decorations adorning the exterior of the airport—wreaths with colorful ornaments on each of the entry doors, Christmas lights that seem to cover the entire surface area of the airport, and poinsettia plants in every corner.

I deadpan, "It's not the most magical thing I've ever seen."

Sharlene smacks my arm. "Rose. Quit. I mean it. We're already here. You might as well enjoy it."

I sigh. "Fine. It's only slightly pretty."

The truth is, the two of us have never seen snow, except on TV when Sharlene forces me to watch holiday movies. I have to admit, being surrounded by a blanket of it is kind of wondrous. But I'm not admitting that to Sharlene. Being impressed by nature isn't the same as celebrating all things Christmas. And knowing Sharlene, she'd take it there.

"That's the spirit," Sharlene says, eyes merry and bright.

This trip is going to feel glacial, both in pace and temperature.

Sharlene points to our left. "Look, here comes one of those cute taxis."

A black, classic car that looks like it drove here straight out of the movie *Grease* approaches us. Hanging off the hood is a Christmas wreath. "Does everything have to scream Christmas?" I mumble when I notice the garland adorning the doors of the car.

"All the car services use classic cars to keep the charm of the town and differentiate that they provide transportation services. Aren't they cute?" Sharlene literally has Christmas trees in her eyes.

"Real cute," I say, sarcasm dripping.

When the car reaches us, the windows roll down, and a stout man with salt-and-pepper hair and an ugly Christmas sweater is in the driver's seat. He's also wearing a Santa hat with a tiny bell at the tip of the triangle. It jingles any time he moves his head. His cherry smile is so wide I wonder if his face hurts.

"Morning, ladies. You two need a ride?"

Sharlene bends down so she can see him better. "We do! We're trying to get to the Holly Oaks Tree Farm."

The driver tips his head. "At your service." He hops out of the car and hurries around to grab our bags, tossing them into his trunk with a thud.

"Thank you so much," Sharlene says as we all slide into the car. "Hurry Home for Christmas" plays low and easy from the stereo.

"What kind of car is this?" I ask. I've seen things like this in movies, but never before have I witnessed it in real life.

The driver grins. "It's a 1949 Dodge Coronet."

Sharlene runs a hand over the soft red fabric. "It's gorgeous."

"Thank ya. Where you from? I'm Adam, by the way," the driver says, glancing at us in the rearview mirror.

"Nice to meet you, Adam. I'm Sharlene, and this is

my sister, Rose." She gestures to me, even though he's got his eyes on the road. "We're actually visiting from Orlando since our parents decided to visit family in Trinidad this year," Sharlene says.

"Orlando, huh. Weather must be a big change for you." He puts his blinker on to turn down one of the quaint town streets. Christmas lights adorn every possible surface area, and snow-covered trees are layered between cottage-style homes—everything an irritating scene copy and pasted from one of those cheesy Christmas movie sets.

"You bet. That and the excessive Christmas decorations," I mutter.

Sharlene squeezes my knee, and I squirm in my seat.

"You'll have to excuse my sister. She's a Christmas Curmudgeon. Guard all your decorations." She gives me a dirty look.

Adam laughs. "No worries at all. Christmas isn't for everyone, but Holly Oaks is a magical place, especially at Christmas. Might even change your mind." He stops at a red light, looks in the rearview, and winks. "Say, you two mentioned your parents went to Trinidad to visit family. Is that where your family is from?"

We both nod and say, "Yes," in unison.

"I've never been there, but I do hope to go one day. At least we get to sample their baked goods."

I wrinkle my eyebrows. "Wait, how?"

"Got our very own Trinidadian bakery here in town. It's called Sugar Cakes. Not too far from here."

Sharlene claps her gloved hands together and places them under her chin. "A Trinidadian bakery here in Holly Oaks? We must go while we're here."

"Best time to go is in the morning. They often sell out quickly. I tell you, I love those coconut dops. Used to eat 'em every morning until my doc told me to take it easy." He chuckles. "But what they're really known for is their sweet bread.

"I haven't had coconut drops in forever," I say.

"I can take you by. It's just a quick detour to the town center. We can probably catch them before all the good stuff is gone."

"Thank you, but we really should get to the tree farm so we can check into our cabin." I look back and forth between him and Sharlene and can't tell who's more excited.

"Come on, Rose. It's not like we have anything to do. We're on *vacation*. We have nothing but time."

"Best sweet bread in town," the driver says. That same cheerful smile that was there when he picked us up returns.

"You mean the only sweet bread in town," I say.

He chuckles again and makes a U-turn.

After a few minutes, Adam pulls into the only parking spot available in front of this so-called Sugar Cakes Bakery. It's a relatively small shop in the town square with a red brick front and a line of people along the entire length of the building.

"You weren't kidding when you mentioned a crowd." I stare at all the people lined up, my eyebrows lifted to the sky.

Adam turns his body to look back at me. "Told ya."

"Should we even bother going in?" I ask.

"That line is standard for Sugar Cakes, but don't worry, it moves pretty quick." He nods in the direction of the shop. "You two can go on, if you want. I don't mind waiting on you."

"Are you sure?" Sharlene asks, but somehow it doesn't quite feel like a question. It's more like she's asking as a formality for something she's already decided.

"A thousand percent sure. And if you want to make it up to me by nabbing me a coconut drop, I wouldn't be opposed." He flashes a smile.

"Deal!" The word rocket launches out of Sharlene's mouth before I can protest. And then she's immediately flinging her door open. I curse her under my breath and get out of the car begrudgingly.

Sharlene races to join the end of the line like her life depends on it, and I follow, thick snow crunching under the winter boots I will only ever wear on this trip.

I grab hold of her arm. "We really should be checking in. We can always try something from here later."

Sharlene scrunches her face. "You heard the driver. No telling when there won't be a line." She takes a few steps. "Besides, it's moving pretty quickly."

I groan and stare up at the sky. A shiver runs through me, and it hits me how much colder it is here than in Orlando. My nose feels like it's turning into its own mini polar region, so I pull my scarf up higher, desperate for any sliver of warmth. Pulling out my phone, I check to see if there are any new emails from potential clients, but there's nothing there.

The bakery is in the middle of the town square. I take in the surrounding shops: Arabella's Gift Shop, Roman's Diner, Off the Rack Bike Shop, and Smoothie Queen. There are a few others with window signs on the other side of the street, but I can't quite make out what they say. After a while, we make it to the inside of the bakery. It smells like Heaven dipped in butter and sugar. My mouth waters as I stare at the glass case of baked goods.

"Okay, not gonna lie, but I'm kind of excited they have everything. Coconut drops, currants rolls, guava pastries, and sweet bread. It's like being in Gran's kitchen at Christmas."

Sharlene is staring up at the menu and gives me a

quick glance before turning her attention back to it. "Right? Good thing I insisted."

"No need to gloat," I say.

She smirks.

"Next!" one of the bakery staff calls. A delicious man with light-brown skin and arresting hazel-green eyes flashes us a dreamy smile. He looks to be about early thirties, just like Sharlene and me. His name tag reads: Ralph. "How can I help you?"

"Good afternoon. Could we have one coconut drop and two currants rolls?"

Ralph holds Sharlene's gaze for a few extra beats than necessary then says, "Of course." He grabs a pastry box and adds our items. Once he closes the box, he sets it on the counter and says, "Haven't seen you around here before. Are y'all on vacation?"

Sharlene smiles. "Yeah. We actually just got in from Orlando, and when our driver said there was a Trinidadian bakery in town, we had to stop and try it for ourselves."

"Best Trinidadian sweets in Holly Oaks," he says with pride.

"Our driver said the same thing, but aren't you the only Trini bakery in town?" Sharlene asks.

"Two things can be true."

Sharlene and Ralph laugh. My eyes bounce back

and forth between the two of them as Sharlene ducks her head with a shy smile. She tucks one of her curls behind her ear while Ralph grins and takes her in. I feel the corner of my mouth lift a tiny bit as I study them. Interesting.

Ralph finally peels his gaze away and types a few things into the register. "We just pulled some fresh currants rolls out of the oven. Should be just a couple minutes. It's going to be $11.95, but take your time. I can put the order on hold."

I look at Sharlene, smirking. "You heard him, Shar. Pay the man."

Sharlene laughs again, this time shaking her head as I bend down and lean in to get a closer look at the baked goods in the display. I don't feel bad at all for making her pay. After all, I'll be eating those delicious currants rolls under duress. She's the one that wanted to stop here. She digs through her purse to retrieve her wallet while I inch my way over until I'm at the very end of the glass display, where there's a half door to the cash wrap area. Just as I straighten my body, the door to the kitchen, which is directly in front of me, swings open, and my eyes connect with...no.

The man entering through the door is holding a large tray of currants rolls, which shakes and almost topples to the floor. He catches it before it does.

My heart stops. Then races. Then stops. I'm trying to work it all out, but it feels like it's been crushed between two cymbals, a little bird flying around the top and all. It vibrates in my chest, fighting desperately to recalibrate.

The pair of eyes widens, refusing to leave mine. They are just like I remember, a mosaic of rich browns.

He's not real, he's not real, I tell myself again and again. I want to close my eyes, but I can't look away either. "Malcom?" I ask. It comes out like a whisper.

"Rose?" Malcolm—the ex-boyfriend who was supposed to be dead to me but has apparently risen—asks.

He's different. Fuller, toned arms, features that look well-traveled, like they've been put to good use in the best way. He's wearing a plain ivory long-sleeved shirt rolled to his elbows, revealing enough of his smooth mahogany skin to know it's still perfect. Nine years looks good on him.

"What are you doing here?" I blurt. It's the only thought that I can put into actual words, because everything else in me spirals out of control. What are the actual odds of Malcolm Sharpe standing in front of me in this random town? Before Sharlene, I had never even heard of this place.

He sets the tray down on the countertop then looks back at me. "Holly Oaks is my home. And I kind of own the place." He points at me. "The better question is, what are *you* doing here?"

His home? How? I want to scream. Because that means we're going to be in the same town for the duration of this trip. Ten days of being afraid he'll be right there when I turn a corner. I side-eye Sharlene. "I was dragged."

Sharlene elbows me then places an arm on my shoulder. "What Rose means is we're on vacation. We were in search of a white Christmas." She pauses. "You seem to be looking and doing well." She's got a big stupid grin on her face as she gestures around the store.

"Thank you. You both look well too."

His eyes stay trained on me, and he's looking at me the same way he always used to—tender but with an intensity only for me. My heart glitches as I get a glimpse of *my* Malcolm, but then I remember I don't know this version. He *was* my Malcolm.

I nod. There isn't much else I can say. It's like my voice has been sucked out of me.

"You've come to the right place for a white Christmas. There's no place like Holly Oaks." He smiles, and my stomach has a familiar chemical reaction. I extinguish it. My stomach better not be getting any ideas. That's not what we're here for.

"So I've heard." It comes out like a grumble, and then there's an awkward pause between everyone. Poor Ralph looks back and forth between Malcolm and me.

Malcolm puts us all out of our misery. "Tell ya what. This is on the house." He taps Ralph on the arm. "Ralph, will you clear the register?"

Ralph lifts his hand to his head and salutes Malcom. "Sure thing, boss."

"Oh, um, you don't have to do that," I say. Because I don't want to owe Malcolm Sharpe anything. We're supposed to be all squared up after the way things ended.

He stands up a little straighter then says, "I want to." His eyes find mine again and stay there. "Welcome to Holly Oaks."

Three

We're nearing the Holly Oaks Tree Farm when I turn to my sister and say, "What are you up to, Sharlene?"

She places a hand on her chest in a dramatic way and says, "Me?"

I narrow my eyes. "Yeah, you. Did you know Malcolm owned that bakery?"

Sharlene presses her lips together, but her lips twitch as she fights a smile.

I, however, am not smiling. I fold my arms over my chest, where my heart is still trying to recover and return to a decent pace. "Sharlene."

She can't fight it anymore, her lips now spreading to

a wide smile. "Okay, fine. I confess. But now that you've seen him, hasn't he aged *very* well?"

"Sharlene! I'm serious. Do I need to remind you that you're the one who wanted me to come on this trip to relax? How am I supposed to do that with Malcolm Sharpe running about?"

She ignores my question, her smile fading. "You know, I've always felt like Malcolm was the one who got away. And Holly Oaks was one of those cute towns I had on my Travel Pinterest board. When I searched and Malcolm's name surfaced, I don't know...it felt like fate."

I sigh. Her heart is in the right place—it always is. "I just wish you would have told me."

She squeezes my arm. "If I told you, would you have come?"

I don't answer.

"Exactly," she says, pleased with herself.

"You're right. No amount of convincing could have gotten me on that plane had I known. But either way, it's been nine years. We've moved on," I say.

She shrugs. "Okay."

All I can do is shake my head.

"We're gonna have a good trip, Malcolm Sharpe or not." She pauses. "Besides, he's a strong, gorgeous, successful man running his own bakery. He's probably so busy and doesn't have time to just hang around." She lifts an eyebrow, a smirk on her face.

I throw both my hands in the air. "You're insufferable."

"I am, but you love me," Sharlene says.

I side-eye her. "After today, that's debatable."

She just keeps that stupid grin on her face. "But you have to admit, he does look good, right?"

I try to hold it in, but a tiny laugh escapes. "How is it fair that he's somehow gotten hotter alongside aging? He should have a potbelly and a receding hairline."

Sharlene's grin morphs into full-blown laughter, which causes a chain reaction. The two of us laugh hard, releasing all the tension I'd been holding in since the bakery.

Our driver, Adam, brings the car to a stop at the front of the Holly Oaks Tree Farm.

It's not what I'm expecting, but the Holly Oaks Tree Farm dazzles. I step out of the car and stare at the rolling hills covered in a blanket of crisp, white snow. Many of those hills are lined with trees. I'll never admit it to Sharlene, but there does feel like something magical is whipping through the air.

Sharlene's head swivels in every direction, her mouth agape. "Wow. It's even better than it is in the pictures."

Once again, I cut her a side look, realizing her premeditated plan.

"Ladies, it's been a pleasure," Adam says. He sets the

second suitcase down.

"Thank you so much for the ride and the detour," Sharlene says.

"Gotta admit, the detour was half selfish." He offers a sheepish smile. "Thanks for the coconut drop."

"Anytime," Sharlene says.

"You two have a wonderful time in our beloved town. If you need a driver, you know where to find me." He opens the car door, slides in, and eases the car away.

Sharlene links an arm in mine. "Let's go check in. I have a feeling this is going to be a great trip."

We approach the main lodge, which is another thing about this town that reminds me of Christmas movies on TV. It's a slightly more modern structure with large glass windows interrupting the vertical reddish wood panels.

Sharlene squeezes my arm as we enter. To my surprise, it's bustling. Not like you'd expect in a city, but more than a little quiet. Just like the exterior of the airport, there are Christmas decorations on every inch. Red. Green. Gold. Cinnamon. Pine. Warm gleaming lights. These are the things that capture my attention first. And. They. Are. Everywhere.

Two people are at the front desk, checking in.

As they turn away and gather their bags, a petite woman behind the desk says, "I hope to see you at the tree lighting tonight. Enjoy your stay!"

"Could this place be any more adorable?" Sharlene asks.

"More like in need of a Christmas intervention," I mumble.

Sharlene jabs me for the second time today.

"Welcome to Holly Oaks Tree Farm," the older woman at the desk says. "How can I help you all today?" She pushes her long salt-and-pepper braid over her shoulder and pushes her tortoise-framed glasses higher up on the bridge of her nose.

Sharlene smiles. "We're just checking in. The reservation should be under the name Douglas."

The woman clicks away on her keyboard for a few seconds, the warm smile on her face never leaving. "Ah, yes, I have you right here." She turns around to a wall of endless keys. Pulling two of them off a hook and placing them in a mini envelope, she slides it across the counter for us to take. "Here you go. If you take the path to the left, you're the last cabin on the right."

Sharlene picks it up. "Thank you so much!"

"I'm Ms. Flores, the owner of the tree farm. We are just thrilled to have you."

"We're thrilled to be here. This place is simply stunning," Sharlene says.

"Thank you." Ms. Flores beams. "It was my late

husband's pride and joy. It's how we met, you know." Her eyes twinkle like they're full of tiny stars.

"Oh yeah?" Sharlene asks, placing her elbow on the counter and leaning in.

"Yes, dear. Our trees are rumored to bring couples together." She says it in a whisper, like it's an ancient secret.

Okay, this woman is clearly off her rocker. No way do I believe that for one second. "Really?" I say, not even bothering to hide the sarcasm in my tone.

If she notices it, Ms. Flores gives no indication. Her dark eyes continue to glimmer. "Oh yes. Mr. Flores accidentally delivered a tree from this very farm to my apartment." This time, the stars in her eyes burst like Christmas fireworks.

"Accidentally?" Sharlene asks, her eyebrows creasing.

I can't believe she's entertaining this.

"Yes. My address was on the order form, but I hadn't placed it. At first, I didn't believe it. But Mr. Flores showed it to me. We never did find out who that order actually belonged to. It was like it appeared out of thin air."

I keep a straight face. "And you think trees did it?"

Ms. Flores just widens her smile, ignoring my skepticism. "Not trees, dear. Christmas magic. The trees are nothing without it." She holds up an index finger in the air.

"Right," I say.

"Well, I think it sounds like it was ordered by fate," Sharlene says.

"That's what I'd like to think." Her eyes flicker, like a memory just surfaced. "Did you see that couple checking in right before you?"

Sharlene and I nod.

"They met here three years ago. We often donate trees to families in need. We have more than enough trees, and it's in alignment with the spirit of Holly Oaks. Anyway, we ask for volunteers sometimes, and the two of them happened to be vacationing with their families when we asked. They saw our call for volunteers, and the rest is history. They're here to celebrate their meet-cute anniversary."

I rock back on my heels, the wooden floorboards creaking underneath. "And let me guess. You have a ton of stories like that?"

"You bet ya." Ms. Flores winks.

"This sounds so enchanting. I don't think we could have picked a better place for a Christmas sisters' trip," Sharlene says.

"Our tree farm *is* quite enchanting. We actually host quite a few of the traditional activities here in our town," Ms. Flores says.

"Like the tree lighting you mentioned to that couple earlier?" Sharlene asks.

Ms. Flores claps. "Yes! You two should come out. It's going to be a great time. And you can't miss my Christmas Eve party either."

What's so great about watching people turn on the lights of a tree? I want to say it out loud, but I also don't want to be rude. Ms. Flores is nice enough—never mind that she believes in magical trees. Plus, I promised Sharlene I'd lighten up. I start to say, "I don't think we have t—"

But Sharlene cuts me out. "It sounds like fun. We've never been to a tree lighting. We'll be there."

A shiver sprints through my body as we enter the cabin we'll be staying in for the next few days. I expect warmth to envelop me, but instead, it's like a punch to the gut when I enter and there's no change. Though the cabin is cold, I do have to admit the vibe is overall cozy. Ms. Flores mentioned the tree farm was fairly old, however everything in the cabin has a modern feel, like it has been updated recently.

I fold my arms and rub them, noting the dark, empty fireplace. "It's just as cold in here as it is outside."

"Oh my goodness, would you look at this place? It's totally living up to all the pictures online," Sharlene says, like she didn't just hear me. Or maybe she's magically become immune to cold weather.

I drop my purse on one of the cozy chairs and place my suitcase upright. "Did those pictures also have a fireplace with no fire?"

Sharlene rolls her eyes at me. "It would be dangerous for them to keep a fire going in here while unattended."

"I mean, central heating was also promised."

Sharlene points to the thermostat next to her. "Here, I'll turn it on. And we can get a fire going too. It will be just like the holiday movies."

I let out a heavy sigh. "That's your problem. As our parents would say, you watch too much TV."

Sharlene chuckles and walks over to the fireplace, where a tented card rests on the mantel.

"Instructions?" I ask.

"Yeah, but..." She searches. "No wood. There's a note here to call the front desk if there isn't any, though."

I glance down at the phone on one of the side tables near the couch. "The number to the main house is right here on this phone. I'll call," I say. I listen to the phone ring a few times. "Hmm. No one is picking up." I hang up.

Sharlene's forehead wrinkles. "That's strange. But it was only Ms. Flores at the front, so maybe she's busy checking someone in."

"It wasn't that far of a walk. I'll head back over and

ask if someone can help," I say.

Sharlene's mouth twists. "You sure? You were the one just complaining about being cold."

I shrug. "I know, but I could use some fresh air." I wouldn't mind the few minutes the short walk would offer me to be alone with my thoughts. I'm still trying to process it, but there's been an internal thunderstorm inside of me since seeing Malcolm at his bakery earlier.

She crosses her arms over her chest. "Fine, but if you're not back in thirty minutes, I'll assume you've been abducted by Christmas spirit and might actually be enjoying yourself."

I want to crack a smile, but I refuse to give her that satisfaction. Instead, I throw her a death stare and head out the door.

Four

On my walk, I listen to the sound of snow crunching and the very loud beating thing in my chest I'm trying desperately to keep at bay. Malcolm Sharpe isn't supposed to be part of the plan. I was supposed to come to Holly Oaks, appease Sharlene, spend some time with my sister, then get back to work. As much beauty as there is around me—those sparkling white hills, evergreen trees, and iridescent sky—I'm now going to be paranoid that I'll run into Malcolm. Maybe he mostly frequents the town. I can stay on property and not participate in those town activities, and I won't see him. Reduce the risk as much as I can.

I feel a little better when I get to the main lodge. As I

pull on the door handle, it doesn't give because someone else is pulling on the other side. Don't people know to keep to the right? I let go, and when it swings open, of course, there he is. I almost lose my footing, but he reaches for me, his hand steadying me at the waist and pulling me closer to him on instinct. I don't want to feel anything, but his citrusy-cedar scent swirls around me and makes me dizzy. What I want is to run straight off this tree farm and get back on a plane to Orlando.

Malcolm's glittery brown eyes search mine from under thick hooded lashes, absorbing me in them the way they always used to. A way that would always make me feel seen and safe. I try to say something, but my words play hide-and-seek in my throat.

Someone coughs, and it's then I notice Ms. Flores standing next to him.

"Are you alright, dear?" she asks.

I straighten, stepping back so Malcolm's hand has no choice but to return to his side where it belongs. "Yes, I'm fine. Just didn't expect to find anyone there." God, what was I saying. It's a public lodge with lots of other guests. Of course there might be people on the other side of the door.

"Sorry, I just got here and was walking Ms. Flores out."

My brain hitches on the words *just got here*. Wait.

"And out I must go. Call me if you need anything.

And will you make sure our guest here is okay?" She smiles at me.

"Hold on. Do you—do you work here?" My stomach doesn't even wait for his answer before it drops.

"You can say that," Malcolm says.

"What does that mean?" I drill my eyes into him.

"Well, technically, I live here. But I help Ms. Flores out. She doesn't have much family left, so I step in when she needs me."

Ms. Flores's eyes bounce back and forth between Malcolm and me. "You two know each other?"

"Used to," I say. I don't mean it to come out so cold, but I also don't regret it either. He doesn't know me anymore. And I don't know him.

His shoulders sink a little. "Rose is an old friend. We went to high school together."

I resist the urge to glare at him. That's what we're calling it. Fine.

That same twinkle from earlier returns in Ms. Flores's eyes. "Interesting. Well, if you're a friend of Malcolm's, then we'll have to give you extra-special Holly Oaks treatment. Right, Malcolm?"

"Absolutely," he says.

I shoot him a glare then give Ms. Flores a warm smile. "That's very sweet, but you really don't have to—"

Ms. Flores cuts me off by holding a hand up.

"Nonsense. It's already done. But I must get going. Malcolm will take care of you."

I watch Ms. Flores leave, and everything slows down. I spin around to face Malcolm and mentally will myself not to get lost in those reckless eyes.

I clear my throat. "I tried calling to get more firewood, but no one answered."

Malcolm nods. "A small disadvantage of the tree farm having a small staff. I can take care of that for you, though." No. I cannot have this man anywhere near me.

"I thought you had to watch the desk? I can follow instructions if you just want to give me the firewood. You don't need to do it for me." The last thing I need is him doing anything for me.

His lips stretch to a smile, and he places a tented sign on top of the check-in counter that reads: *We'll be right back*. "Seriously, it's no problem. I'm always happy to do anything for you, Rose."

He holds my gaze, and I try to look away, but I can't. And now I'm remembering the way I always felt like his eyes had tiny magnets made for mine.

Our walk back to my cabin is mostly quiet with a side of awkward. Once we're at the front door, Malcolm places the wagon of firewood he's been pulling off to the side and piles a few neat bundles of logs into his hands.

When I reach for one at the same time as him, his fingers accidentally cover mine. I gasp, as if they've just scorched my skin, and pull my hand away. But Malcolm curls his fingers into his palm and looks over at me.

He clears his throat. "I got this."

I don't argue and instead push the key into the cabin's door. A chill slips down my spine when we're on the other side. "Don't know how you live here in this freezing weather. I've never missed my warm sunshine so much."

Malcolm makes his way to the fireplace and places the bundles of logs down. "You get used to it."

"Sharlene?" I call, walking around.

Silence.

"If she's anything like the Sharlene of past, I'll bet she's gone exploring or looking for somewhere to read."

I want to make a slick comment about him not knowing anything about us anymore but remember he's helping me out. Instead, I pull out my phone and see a text from Sharlene.

Sharlene: *Just checking out this gorgeous property. Back soon*!

I click the screen off and put it away. "Looks like

you're right."

Malcolm chuckles as he piles the wood into the fireplace. "Some things never change. She always loved both adventure and reading when we were kids."

"I guess so. The opposite of me."

He nods. "You were always so..."

"Cautious?"

We both smile.

"It's not necessarily a bad thing. Just as long as you take risks when it matters." He eyes me then goes back to the logs.

I fold my arms. "I don't mind risks. I just prefer there be a plan attached."

He laughs and shakes his head.

I pause, debating on whether to continue talking. I could just go inside and pretend to busy myself with literally anything else. But something in me wants to know more about his life here, so I ask, "Seems like you're great at taking risks. How'd you end up in Holly Oaks, anyway?"

He holds a lighter to the stacked wood, and a fire sparks to life. "After I left culinary school, I was searching for a place to call home. Orlando reminded me too much of Mum, and things weren't great between Dad and me since Mum died, as you know."

I swallow. Things were shaky when he left school.

I imagine they didn't get better when he stopped coming home.

"Has it been long since you talked to him?" I ask.

He casts his gaze to the floor. "It's been a few years. But I found a home here. Ms. Flores was looking for a chef for the lodge kitchen. Got the listing from a classmate of mine who grew up here."

"So you got your start here?"

Malcolm nods. "Yeah. And when the chance to own the bakery came up, I had enough experience and money saved to really go for it. Even took a couple business classes online."

I pause for a few seconds. "Just like that?"

"Just like that. My gut knew what was up. Told me to take the risk—so I listened." The fire blazes and crackles in front of him.

It's something I've always admired about him—the way he knew what he wanted when it came to his career, and the way he could just jump to get it. I just wished back then he would apply that to his relationships. Wish he'd taken the risk on us.

I swallow. "My gut wants me to take risks all the time, but it's hard to listen."

"Maybe you just need some practice." He meets my eye but looks away. "Did Ms. Flores tell you and Sharlene about the tree lighting tonight?"

"She did," I say.

"And what does your gut say?" he asks.

I grin. "My gut says I should stay in the confines of this warm, cozy cabin instead of standing out in the biting cold to look at debatably pretty lights."

He laughs, and it rumbles through me, an attempt to wake sleeping butterflies. I put an end to it before he can.

"Maybe we should listen to my gut this time." He points to his stomach.

"And what does *your* gut say?" I challenge.

"That you should start taking risks by coming to the tree lighting. It's actually low risk and pretty magical." He stands and faces me.

I narrow my eyes and tilt my head to the side. My eyes skim the cuts of muscle outlining his arms as they peek through his fitted sweater.

He smiles, and everything solid in me dissolves, reduced to something molten and malleable. This is why I can't let this man get too close again. There is power in his eyes, in his presence, in his...lips. I immediately snuff that thought out.

"There'll be hot chocolate," he says, interrupting my thoughts.

It's annoying the way he still knows me so well. "Fine. But only because I'll risk anything for hot chocolate.

Five

ehildren zigzagging with messy clumps of snow in their gloved hands. Old-fashioned carts in a straight line serving Christmas favorites. Townspeople standing in clusters with warm drinks in their hands while the soft din of their conversations and laughter float above us. A twenty-foot-tall verdant tree, lush and ribboned, waiting to be all lit up. The scent of pine and chocolate and fresh mountain air. This is apparently the Holly Oaks way when it comes to a tree lighting.

Once we make it to the main cabin for the event, I wonder how, for the second time, someone has dragged me somewhere I don't necessarily have the desire to be.

It's twenty degrees, and people think it's wise to stand outside for lights and merriment. Make it make sense. I shove my hands further into my coat pockets, like it will somehow keep me warm, but it's no use.

I lean over and whisper to Sharlene, "All these people showed up just to watch them turn on the lights of a tree for the first time this season?"

Wonder glazes over Sharlene's eyes. "Yeah, isn't it marvelous? We've never seen anything like this except on TV." She points at everything around us: the hot chocolate and food stands, the people socializing with cups in their hands, the colossal tree.

I shake my head. "You're serious?"

"Just imagine when they actually turn on the lights. There's going to be magic zipping all around us."

"The only magic I want to see is the magic of a fire sparking in that fireplace when we get back to our cabin."

Sharlene laughs. "I mean, I'm not opposed to that idea. But let's not miss out on the magic that's already where we are. And you could stand to loosen up a bit. You promised you would."

I shrug. "Must have been something in the eggnog."

She tries to scowl, but it becomes a smirk. We make our way closer to the tree, where everyone is gathered.

"I'm so glad you made it," Ms. Flores says when she spots us. She's bundled in a thick coat and fuzzy scarf

36

that wraps from her neck all the way up to just under her eyes.

"Me too! This tree is incredible," Sharlene says, craning her head up to where the tree meets sky.

Ms. Flores stares at the tree. "Mr. Flores loved this tradition. He said we had so much beauty here, and there was no reason we shouldn't share it with the rest of the town. It's why so many people feel at home here."

"That's very generous. He sounds like he was a wonderful man," Sharlene says.

Ms. Flores gives her arm a quick squeeze. "He had a big heart."

I'm about to join the conversation when Malcolm interjects. "He sure did. His legacy lives through this entire tree farm."

My head whips in his direction, and he flashes me a smile when our eyes meet. In his hands is a carrier containing four cups.

"There's one other person I know with a heart just as big." Ms. Flores beams at Malcolm.

She's not wrong. He always had a big heart, and I—being a researcher of all things Malcolm—discovered after my experiment that he was capable of big love—he just never really knew what to do with it.

Malcolm blushes, and my heart slips up. I forgot how insanely attractive he looks when someone gives him a compliment that makes him uncomfortable. He begins handing the cups out. He starts with Ms. Flores, then one for Sharlene, and then...me. I move in slow motion to take it.

He leans in. "And here's the only reason you decided to take a risk and attend."

"Hot chocolate over everything," I say, holding my cup up.

He clinks his against mine, even though there's no real clink. "Cheers."

"Cheers," I say and take a sip. This is not any hot chocolate. It's the richest, creamiest kind that's so sweet it cuts your throat. "Oh my gosh, that's good. I don't think I've ever had hot chocolate this good."

Malcolm laughs, and I'm in dangerous territory again. He stares at me and—wait, is he staring at my lips? It's all too familiar, and I contemplate heading for those rolling hills in the distance.

He takes the slightest step closer to me, and on instinct, I jerk back.

"Sorry," he says. "It's just...you have..."

But I've already felt the stickiness of what the warm drink left behind. "Whipped cream on my lips?" I finish the sentence for him. "If you don't end up with a little whipped cream on your lips, you're not doing it right." I try to lick my lips, but I know I'm not successful, because

I can still feel it.

Malcolm reaches out, and his thumb does a slow sweep over my lips to remove it. He takes his time, our eyes interlocking. Why the hell isn't he wearing gloves? If he were, my stomach wouldn't be flipping.

"Um, thank you." It sputters out of me. Oh no. None of this is supposed to be happening. I glance at Sharlene, who stares back at me, an eyebrow raised in both question and delight.

Ms. Flores's voice cuts into my thoughts. "I hope this isn't the last lighting."

Malcolm places a hand on her shoulder. "Don't worry, the right buyer will come along. They will love our traditions, and they will love this town, just like we do."

Ms. Flores pats his hand where it rests on her shoulder.

Someone taps the mic then, and all heads turn toward a podium next to the tree. A medium-height woman with a bob of dark hair faces the crowd with the cheeriest of smiles. "Good evening," she says to the crowd.

Some people respond, "Good evening, Mayor Gregory!"

"It's lovely to see you all here for our annual tradition. We'll always be grateful to Mr. Flores for taking over this tradition in a time where we struggled for support." She pauses and grins. "Plus, it takes a lot of pressure off of me."

Everyone laughs.

"I grew up in this town, and the tree lighting has always

been one of my favorite traditions. I could probably gush about that all night and tell you a hundred stories, but I know you're all probably thinking, *please don't.*"

More laughter from the audience fills the air.

Mayor Gregory smiles. "It's much too cold for that. May I have the clicker, please?" A man in a bright-purple puffy coat makes his way to the podium and hands her a little black box. She holds it up in a dramatic fashion. "Prepare to be dazzled, everyone! Three, two...one."

Click. White lights spring to life, illuminating the red, gold, and glittery ornaments. I don't mean for it to happen, but a gasp slips out. Somehow, Malcolm ends up behind me. He's so close I can feel the heat emanating from his body, instantly setting me on edge.

He leans in, his lips inches from my ear. "See? I knew you'd like it." His voice is intimate and rich, reminding me of all the secrets we used to exchange.

The hairs on the back of my neck stand on end, and my breath hitches from the closeness. And when I turn my head the slightest bit, there he is, pupils blown wide and gazing at me. "Who says I like it?" I mean it to come out confident, but instead, the words are unsteady.

"Oh, you do." He smirks. "Besides, I know you, and I know what you like."

I feel a tiny bit of that wall I built specifically for Malcolm Sharpe shake, a brick let loose. How dare he show up with his tiny earthquakes. That isn't supposed to happen.

"I can also see on your face that a million things are swirling up here." He points to my head. "But tell me you didn't just enjoy the moment."

I try to fight a smile. Why is it so easy for him to disarm me?

"Just say it." He's still grinning, daring me to lie to him.

My lips waver until they finally betray me. "I always did hate when you were right—which wasn't often."

He bursts out laughing. "Oh okay. I see how it is."

"But yeah, I'm really glad I took the risk."

"I knew it," he says.

"So, is there anything to do in Holly Oaks that's not related to Christmas?" I ask.

He lets out a deep laugh. "Not in this town." He pauses for a beat then says, "I've really missed you."

There goes my heart again, beating in retrograde and with hope that I intentionally extinguished when I realized we were on different paths. For a moment, it feels like we're the previous versions of ourselves, every black and white memory springing to life in vibrant color. The Rose and Malcolm of all those Christmases past. But then I remember this isn't then. This is now, and we are not the same two people. I try not to, but I allow myself a thought: Maybe that's not such a bad thing.

Six

The sound of my room door slamming against the wall snatches me out of my warm, comfortable slumber. I bolt up, and Sharlene is standing in the doorway with a grin so wide it reaches her eyes.

I groan and plop back down, covering my head with my pillow. "Go away."

"Oh no, no, no." She makes her way to the window on the other side of the room and flings the curtains open. "Rise and shine, it's Christmas shopping time!"

I peek out from under my pillow as sunlight streams in. The clock on the wooden side table near my bed says 8 a.m. "Seriously, Shar? The stores aren't even open right now." I pull the comforter up over my shoulders and settle back in.

Not only are stores not open, but I hardly slept at all with all the restless energy burning through me. My mind kept opening every Malcolm memory I had on file: Our first kiss in the back of his pickup one night when we were looking up at stars. The night we shopped together for gifts at The Orlando Christmas Market, and he got the call about his mom in the middle of our food-truck dinner. The way I held him in that hospital hallway when everything was final, and he couldn't hold his pain in anymore. When he told me out of nowhere that he was moving away for culinary school. How he said we should take a break and put us on pause right before Christmas. How days stretched into weeks, then months, until finally we were strangers. How the heartbreak was like a slow-moving snowstorm that wrecked me while all I could do was wait it out.

Sharlene's voice rattles my thoughts. "But we have to grab breakfast first. Besides, we can explore while we wait. And something tells me people are up much earlier in small towns."

I cannot figure out why she has so much energy. "We're supposed to be on va-ca-tion. Did you forget what the very definition of the word means?"

"All it means is time spent away from home," Sharlene says.

"Exactly. Time spent away from home, resting and relaxing."

"You can do that at home."

"Not really," I grumble. "Hence the need for a vacation."

She flings the comforter off me just like she did with the curtains. "Come on, Rose. I want to explore the town. I haven't even started my Christmas shopping yet.

I roll onto my back. "You can just give me the gift of extra time to sleep."

She shakes her head. "Get up. I'll be waiting for you in the living room."

I sigh as the door clicks shut.

I admit I didn't want to get out of bed. However, the smell of fresh coffee when we enter the main house makes me immediately glad that Sharlene insisted. My mouth waters as the strong hazelnut aroma fills me up.

We make our way to the dining room and stop in our tracks. Malcolm has a hand resting on one of Ms. Flores's shoulders. Her eyes are watery, and she's looking off to the side.

I'm hesitant, but I say, "Morning."

Ms. Flores straightens up and wipes the corner of her eye when she sees us. She smiles, but it's weak. "Hello, dears. How was your first night at Holly Oaks?"

"Never slept better," Sharlene says.

I side-eye her. "Yeah…just wish I could have slept in a little longer."

Ms. Flores offers another weak smile. "I'm happy to hear it was comfortable for you."

"Is everything okay?" I ask. She looks down, so I look at Malcolm.

Malcolm clears his throat. "We just got some bad news."

I raise an eyebrow. "What news?"

Ms. Flores looks up at Malcolm. My chest squeezes at their exchange. I know how hard he took it when his mom passed away, and in the small time that I've witnessed their interactions, it seems like Ms. Flores has been able to fill that supporting role.

She sighs. "It turns out some of the trees aren't doing so well. We're used to not all the trees surviving, but right now, the number of dying trees seems to be increasing at a higher rate than usual."

"Oh," I say. I know it's not good, but I'm not entirely sure what that means for her.

"That's not going to be good for the sale of the tree farm." Malcolm locks his jaw.

He always knew what I was thinking. I study the edge of his jaw and remember how it felt under my fingers when I traced it before leaning in for a kiss. I shake the thought away.

"I did hear you mention that last night," I say.

Ms. Flores forces another smile. "I'm not as young as I used to be. About six months ago I decided it was time to sell the Holly Oaks Lodge and Tree Farm. I don't have any children, and I can't keep up with the maintenance." I don't know her at all, but I feel a slight ache from the anguish in her voice.

Malcolm steps in to give her a timeout. "So far, there's only been one interested buyer that might be open to the idea of keeping the lodge the same. And there's an offer on the table. We don't want to lose our town traditions, but holding out for the perfect buyer is a lot for her too."

Sharlene tilts her head to one side. "Isn't there anything you can do to turn the trees around to ensure the sale? Maybe even slow it down?"

Malcolm nods. "That's what we're hoping to do. We're waiting to hear more info from one of Ms. Flores's farmhands now."

Sharlene turns to me. "Rose, maybe you can check it out?"

I hold both my hands up. "Trees really aren't my specialty."

Sharlene turns back to Ms. Flores and Malcolm but points at me. "She's being modest." Her attention is back on me. "Everyone knows you're the plant whisperer. A tree is just a giant plant. You never know. Maybe you can suggest a solution for them to try at the very least."

"I don't think—" I stop when I catch Ms. Flores's eye and then Malcolm's. Trees aren't plants, despite what Sharlene thinks, but the looks on their faces make it difficult to say no. I start again, trying to soften my words. "Look, I really would like to help, but I'm not sure how much good it will do. I've never really worked with trees."

Malcolm speaks up. "But you're closer to answers than any of us are. Besides, something tells me you could probably figure out how to fix it."

When I look up, his deep brown eyes are focused on me. At first, I think he's joking, but his eyes hold nothing but genuine admiration. I don't have time to work that out now, but it feels like an intervention—one my heart didn't ask for.

My gaze forges a path through each of their faces, and I sigh. "Okay. I'll take a look. But you all have to promise not to be disappointed if I can't help."

They each nod.

"Of course," Ms. Flores says, shifting her attention to Malcolm. "Will you take her to the west end?"

Malcolm nods. "Yeah. Let me just text Ralph to make sure he's up for handling things at the bakery."

Panic rises all the way up to my throat. "Wait. Right now?" I glance at Sharlene. "We were supposed to go shopping and—"

"Of course. All good," Sharlene cuts me off. I curse her in my mind for always wanting to be so helpful—a trait she inherited from our father.

"We can go after," she says, reaching into her purse and pulling out a romance novel. "I always keep a book in my purse. I'll curl up by the fire and wait here until you get back."

I do not return her smile. It's funny how I'm the one who wanted to chill and relax, and she gets to stay behind and cozy up by the fire. Mentally, I hit her in the face with a pillow just as I did when we were kids and she annoyed me.

Malcolm walks back our way once he ends his call. "Ready to go?" he asks.

I'm not sure ready is the right word.

I look up at the glass boxes moving along on a thin wire against the backdrop of mountains like monuments. He's not serious. Malcolm Sharpe cannot be serious.

I take a step back from him. "Hold on. You want me to get on that makeshift flying contraption?"

He chuckles. "Makeshift flying contraption? It's called a gondola."

"I don't care what it's called. It's way too high and looks way too heavy for that wire."

Malcolm laughs, clearly having the time of his life over my genuine concern for safety. "They've been stuck before, but since I've been here, we've never had any accidents."

So, what? They've had accidents before he got here? My heart picks up pace in my chest. I bite my bottom lip. "Can't we take a snow mobile or something?"

"I checked. There aren't any available right now." His gaze drops to my lips for a quick second—right where my bottom one is caught under my teeth.

"It doesn't look safe," I say in one last attempt to wiggle my way out of getting on that thing.

He takes a step toward me. His hand raises, then drops, and I wonder if he was thinking of reaching for me—just like he always did when I needed comforting. "Rose. I wouldn't put you in harm's way. A lot of time has passed. But there's one constant, and it's that I will always, always, keep you safe."

Butterflies I thought were dead rise, their wings fluttering, fluttering, fluttering through my stomach, disobeying what my brain screams at them: *Stop. Stop. Stop.* I look at a mass of mountains in the distance, and again, I want to run in their direction.

Malcolm holds out a hand for me to take. "Do you

trust me?"

For a few seconds, I just look down at it. Do I? I used to. But it's like he just said. A lot of time has passed. But it's Malcolm. I might not trust him with my heart again, but I do trust that he'd keep me safe. So I reach for his hand. What I'm not expecting is the way it charges and tingles, electric in a way only Malcolm's energy can make it. What I'm not expecting is for those darn butterflies to become electric too. They are wild and urgent, bursting past barriers and spreading through me like they've just been waiting to continue the mission. As his large hands take hold of mine, the feeling of safety is confirmed.

Malcolm leads me to where the operator waits. They exchange a brief greeting, though it all feels like a blur, and everyone is under ice water. My brain goes into overdrive from the kaleidoscope of emotions shifting through me.

Malcolm steps onto the gondola first, still holding my hand. "Take the risk," he says, his voice soft and warm.

I take a step and then another. I'm on the gondola. There's a long seat behind us, so I quickly sit down before I can change my mind. Malcolm lets go of my hand and sits on the other end. Meanwhile, I'm trying to regulate my breathing.

When it starts moving, I grip the edge of the seat with two hands. "Are you sure this is safe?" I manage to get out. My brain can rationalize that he's already told me he wouldn't put me in harm's way, but I can't help but ask it again anyway.

He gives me an easy smile. "Yes. I've been on these a thousand times. Plus, we run inspections on them often to make sure they're good to go for guests.

My eyes travel to the window I'm sitting next to. I let out a deep breath as we glide over trees, cabins, and snow. That would be a long way down if these wires snapped.

"So what's the real reason you're in Holly Oaks?" Malcolm asks, interrupting my cooked-up crisis.

"The truth is that I didn't want to come at all," I tell him.

He raises both eyebrows like I've offended him.

"Sharlene insisted I needed a change of scenery. We didn't land a dream client that would have been a big move for Plant Ladies."

"I'm so glad you made Plant Ladies happen." He pauses. "Dream client, huh. Fern Gardens?"

Again, my heart falters. "You remember?"

"You loved that place and talked about working with them all the time."

I wouldn't have imagined he'd remember that.

"I can't help but feel like a failure. It's been nine years, and we're still not where I've envisioned this business going. Even though Gran's not here, I just wanted to make her proud, and I can't even do that." I look out at the mountains against the gray-blue sky.

"Who says she wouldn't be proud?" he asks.

"Weren't you listening? I haven't been able to get to where I want to be."

"I'm pretty sure she'd be proud of you. You and Sharlene started your own thing. You know how many people want to do that and don't?" He pauses for a second, as if debating whether or not to say more. "Besides, you're so much more than a career and clients, Rose. That's not what I see at all when I look at you."

I swallow, and our eyes lock. "What do you see?" It's out before I have the chance to think better of asking.

"I see a smart, caring, insanely attractive woman who just happens to have a green thumb."

I have words somewhere. They're scrambled in my throat, though, and I'm trying desperately to sort them out. He's not supposed to be saying things like this to me—not anymore.

"Besides," he continues, "sometimes we think we want something, but the universe shows us another path." He looks away and studies the trees on the other side of the window.

Like us? Like the way I wanted him but never quite knew if that was truly mutual? He cared about me; I always knew that. But did he love me? Did he want me the same desperate way I wanted him? Maybe he realized I wasn't on his path because the universe showed him another way.

At last, I say, "I'm not sure what that path is. I put all my eggs in that basket. Now I don't know what I'm supposed to do next."

"More eggs can always be made," he says. "Your gran always believed you could run your own business. I'm sure she'd still have no doubt that you'll figure things out.

"Maybe I'm just not ready for the success I'm dreaming of."

"Are we really ever ready for anything?" he asks.

"Maybe not. I certainly wasn't ready to be rejected by Fern Gardens."

"Maybe that rejection is just redirection. Think of it as a good thing. Maybe something even better is waiting for you." He meets my gaze. For a second, we just look at each other. And I don't fight anything, just let myself soak in all things Malcolm. When I realize I'm staring, I blink, my cheeks heating.

"For what it's worth, I know you'll figure it out. You always do."

If my cheeks were heating before, they burst into flames now. He was always so good at seeing me. "Thanks, Malcolm."

He grins. "Just reminding you of who you are—and how special that green touch is."

"All thanks to Gran. She taught me that plants can grow and feel, just like us."

"That they can live and die, just like us," he finishes.

The corner of my mouth quirks up. "You really do have a good memory, don't you?"

"I could never forget your gran's wisdom—or you." He studies me for a few beats before looking away.

My butterflies from the grave lose their marbles again, flap their wings in chaos. It's then I realize something: this is all too familiar. He always did this—said something, then countered it with an action that made me wonder if he really meant it. I watch him carefully, reminding myself not to fall under his spell again.

Just as I make up my mind, the gondola stops, then shakes, and I lift off my seat slightly. Malcolm's body crashes into mine. I'm pressed against the window, one of his hands against the glass behind me to steady himself. We are close. We are touching. I am touching Malcom Sharpe after years of not touching Malcolm Sharpe. Not only are his eyes on me but everything else is. My mind catches on his citrus and cedar scent. All my thoughts halt then scatter as I try to take back control of them. His eyes again find my lips, and now I can't seem to regulate my breathing. He inhales, exhales, inhales, exhales.

And then, at last, he says, "Sorry." But it's the kind of sorry that has no remorse. Like a *sorry not sorry*. He pushes off the glass and backs away until he's back on his side of the seat.

That's the thing about spells. You can fall under them even if you don't want to.

Seven

When we're finally able to get off the gondola, I don't feel like the same Rose that got on. Malcolm again offers a hand—this time to help me off. The contact is hazardous, but we're both wearing gloves, so I take it.

Snow crunches under my boot when I take the first step. Somewhere in the distance, birds chatter, and the sun remains tucked behind pillowy clouds. I stare out at the endless trees in the distance.

"We're definitely not in Kansas anymore." I push a loose curl back into the hood of my coat as I scan the area. "That's a lot of trees. I mean, I saw them in the distance when we were back at the cabins, but seeing them stretch on for miles feels like we just stepped into a different world."

"Beautiful, right?"

When I peel my eyes off the trees, he's looking at me. I nod and move my gaze back to the expanse of green.

"Ms. Flores likes to call it her very own winter wonderland. It's what Mr. Flores used to tell her. He actually tried to pitch it as a bonus when he proposed to her."

"That has to be the sweetest thing I've ever heard," I say.

"Yeah. And she said it was a nice bonus, but she would have married him even without the promise of a wonderland," he says.

"My heart can't take any more. It's going to liquify right here." I chuckle. It reminds me of my mother and father too. They fell in love at eighteen and are still together. I want a love like that.

"Come on. It's this way," Malcolm says.

We head down a row of trees. It only takes a few steps before I see the needles peppering the blanket of snow. I remove one of my gloves, stoop down, and pick up a few. I roll them between my fingers then lean in to study them in my palm. I look at the tree and touch some of the branches, repeating the process as I study the dry, yellowing needles.

"You're not doing so well, are you?" I ask. Gran always said that things that grew—plants, trees, flowers—could hear us. She took care of her plants every single day and held whole conversations with them.

"Any ideas?" Malcolm asks.

"Maybe. I don't want to make an assumption before I have a chance to research, but I have a hunch what might be going on here," I say, glancing around at all the trees. "Needle cast disease."

Malcolm wrinkles his brows. "Disease?"

"Yeah. I'll need to do some more research. Like I said, this really isn't my wheelhouse. But look at all these needles." I point down the aisle at all the needles under each tree. "They're dropping at a rapid pace. A tree naturally loses needles, but not like this. Something is definitely wrong."

"I think that's what we were afraid of." His shoulders hunch.

I gently take one of the branches and stretch both my hands out beneath it. "See the color of the needles?"

Malcolm leans in, squinting at the branch in my hands. "Mm-hmm."

Again, I'm not prepared for the way my body insists on reacting when he's that close. I can feel the air buzzing where I end and he begins. I steady my voice. "The yellowish color at the tips is an indication of this particular disease. Plus..." I look around again, letting my eyes linger over some individual trees.

"Plus, what?" Malcolm asks.

"This disease can occur when the trees are planted too close to each other," I say.

Malcolm folds his arms and looks into the distance. "We did that to increase the profits per acre."

"Yeah, but the dense foliage can't withstand too much humidity, and humidity increases when there isn't enough space between them."

For a minute, he doesn't say anything. I know him well enough to know he's trying to calm himself down internally. He swallows then clears his throat. "That sounds like a grave mistake. Can it be fixed?"

"I honestly don't know. The disease can spread, so it depends on how much. Granted, if I remember correctly, if it hasn't spread too much, you can remove the affected branches."

Malcolm lets out a deep breath and sticks his hands in his pockets. "So what's next? How do we even begin to try to fix this?"

There's a little panic there, though he tries to hide it.

"The next step is getting your farm hands to run an assessment of the spread. We need to first figure out what we're dealing with. And then I'll have to look up if there's a solution." *We?* When did I adopt this problem?

"I'll call as soon as we get back to the main house."

I nod, turning to make my way back down the row of trees we're tucked between.

"Rose?" Malcolm asks.

I look back at him over my shoulder. "Yeah?"

His lips break into an easy smile. "I knew you'd figure it out."

"Let's see if I'm right first."

"You always are."

Heat builds under the skin of my cheeks, a stark contrast to the icy air pushing against the surface. I smile back at him.

"Before we head back to the main house, can I take you somewhere?"

I narrow my eyes. "Is it over the rainbow?"

He laughs, and the sound slips past my defense wall, making it all the way to my heart.

"It's not exactly somewhere over the rainbow, but it's close to it."

My brain begs *don't do it*, but I say, "Okay," anyway.

It's not what I'm expecting. We're up high, and even though I wanted to have words with the gondola initially, I'm thankful it was able to give us a lift. Getting up here by foot would have likely made me grinchier.

In front of me are stretches of mountains covered in glittering snow against the canvas of a dusky blue sky. The air feels different too. More pure. Like you can taste the oxygen.

"It's...it's stunning." I can't manage anything else. I could take a picture of it, and it'd never be enough to capture the exact view or feeling.

Malcolm stares into the distance like he's in a daze. "It never gets old. I come up here when I need to clear my head or when I need a moment of peace. Maybe it's because it's up so high, but it makes me feel closer to my mom."

I don't know what makes me do it, but I put a hand on his shoulder. "I still think about her often, you know. And if she saw you now, I think she'd be proud of you."

"You think so?" he asks. His voice is barely a whisper.

"I know it. I remember when she'd encourage you to keep working on your baking skills, even when..." I trail off, realizing my mistake.

"Even when Dad didn't?" he asks.

I take my hand off his shoulder. "I'm sorry. I didn't mean to—"

"It's fine. I've made my peace with it. I'm just glad I listened to my mother instead of him."

We're quiet for a few beats, and I debate whether to

ask more. "You mentioned it had been a while since you last talked to him. Any plans to change that?"

He doesn't answer right away. For a second, I wonder if he's angry at me for bringing it up.

He clears his throat. "Nope. No plans."

"I take it he didn't approve of you opening the bakery?"

Malcolm sighs. "I don't think he knows I own a bakery. He wanted me to take over his construction business, as you might recall. And I went off to culinary school instead. He said I was ruining his legacy. Doubt he'd want to hear anything about my bakery."

"Maybe he'd be proud if he could see what you've done. Owning a bakery is a big deal, Malcolm. It's not an easy field."

Malcolm shakes his head, shoves his hands in his pockets. He glances at me then back out at the mountains. "You know, there was a time I thought I could impress him. I was gonna expand the bakery, make Sugar Cakes a household name. And now that I have the chance to do just that, I don't think it would matter at all to him."

My eyes widen. "Expansion is on the table for Sugar Cakes?"

The corner of his mouth quirks up. "Yeah. We're talking to distributors now. They've already presented a distribution deal." He says this like it's no big deal.

I slap his arm. "Malcolm. That's fantastic. I always

had a feeling your cakes would make it big. You gonna take the deal?"

He shrugs. "Thinking about it."

I fold my arms and tap my chin. "What's the thing you've been drilling into my brain again?" I continue to tap my chin and wrinkle my forehead. "Oh yeah. Take the risk."

He laughs, and it thunders in my heart, electric. It whispers how much it wants to live off that sound.

"Shoot. I wasn't expecting to have my own advice turned back around on me."

"You can't dish it and then not take it," I say. "But in all seriousness, Sugar Cakes should be a household name. You should take the risk—with your brand and your dad."

"Maybe." He pauses and turns to me, a mischievous look in his eyes. A montage of memories flashes in my brain as I think of him looking at me that way when we were us.

"Why are you looking at me like that?" I ask.

"Because right now, I'm going to focus on taking another risk."

Do. Not. Move. Butterflies. "What's that?"

"This!" He picks up a handful of snow and rolls it into a sloppy ball. He stretches his hand back like a pitcher on a baseball team.

"Don't you d—" I try to warn. But it's too late because he launches the snow at me before I can finish.

I pick up my own handful and throw it at him, but he dodges.

"Wait until I catch you, Malcolm Sharpe!" I shout, my voice vibrating in the quietness around us.

We hurl snow at each other again and again until we're both freezing and tired. Until there's nothing left to do but head back.

Eight

After spending so much time with Malcolm, assessing the trees, and then our impromptu snowball fight, I arrived back to the main lodge as a human icicle. Sharlene finally took pity on me and agreed that I deserved a Christmas cookie and relaxation for the rest of the day. I couldn't stop thinking about the trees, though—or Malcolm. One of those things would get me into trouble—and I didn't come to Holly Oaks looking for trouble.

In a comfy plaid wingback chair at the main house, I open my laptop to start my research on needle cast disease the following day. The fireplace crackles in front of me while behind me people wander in and out with their morning coffee. It's been less than twenty-four hours, so I'm not sure the extent of the spread, but I still need to make sure I'm on the right track.

Scrolling through several articles, I'm convinced I am, in fact, right. Once I'm fairly confident, I start to look for solutions. I let out a deep breath when I learn there isn't much.

I do find a tree medicine solution that kills the disease in addition to stopping the spread. I email the link to myself so I can show Ms. Flores. Just as I email it, a new message bubble pops up in the corner of my screen.

"Probably a formal rejection," I mutter.

"Rejection?" a voice says over the back of the chair.

I jump at Malcolm's lush voice, nearly toppling my laptop. I catch it in time, though, then X out of the email tab. "It's nothing."

Malcolm stares down at me, his eyes half puzzle, half concern. "Okay..." He pauses then says, "Hey, I just wanted to thank you for helping out yesterday. Otis, our lead farmhand, is already on it."

"Of course. I'm glad I could offer some insight." I tell him about what I just found and point to the screen. "This may work to restore the needles over time too." He leans in. Again: cedar, citrus, Malcolm, butterflies. It's a chain reaction.

"That looks great. I'll let Ms. Flores and Otis know.

Maybe we can get an order going soon."

"I just want to be clear that none of this is guaranteed, but I think we might have caught it in time for the treatment to work." I shut my laptop.

"Thank you, Rose," Malcolm says. When I look up at him, he hasn't moved. His eyes glitter under the soft lighting of the lodge.

"Of course," I say, forcing my eyes away from his. "Should we exchange numbers in case anything comes up?"

He tilts his head to the side, like he's confused. But it clears as it sinks in that I don't have his number anymore. "Right." Pulling his phone from his pocket, he types out a text.

My phone dings, and my mouth falls open in surprise. "You still have my number?"

He nods, a longing flickering across his face. I offer a small smile. It's all I have left as I process that he never deleted my number. Me, on the other hand? I erased every trace of him.

"So, you ready for another risk?" Mischief returns to his gaze.

I narrow my eyes and cross my arms. "What are you up to?"

"There's another Christmas activity tonight." He lifts an eyebrow.

"You all are really living up to that title of Christmas

capital, huh?" I say.

He chuckles. "It's not a title. It's a fact."

I laugh. "So what's the activity?"

"It's a sweet bread bakeoff." He smirks.

I gasp. "Sweet bread?" I used to spend so many winters helping Gran bake sweet bread.

"That's right. It's a tradition I started." He pauses. "And have also won every year too."

"So, what, you want a cookie?" I roll my eyes but keep my smirk.

"I don't want a cookie. But I do want to know if you're in," he says.

I throw my head back and laugh as hard as I can. "If I were in, I'd wreck your record. You know I have Gran's recipe."

"I've had a lot of years to practice. And a beloved bakery as a receipt," he challenges.

"This time, practice does not make perfect. No way you can beat Gran's sweet bread."

He leans in closer. "Prove it."

"I don't have to prove a thing to you, Malcolm Sharpe."

"You forfeiting?"

"How can I forfeit if I wasn't ever competing?"

"I'll just have to continue my title of Sweet Bread King, then."

I shake my head. "Self-proclaimed."

"Tell it to the town." He drills his eyes into me. "Come on, I'll even let you use my kitchen."

I pause and study him. What would be his motive for getting me to enter a sweet bread competition?

"What is it? Fear of taking the risk?" he asks, knowing full well that word hits a nerve with me.

"You know what? You're on."

After my research session, I meet Sharlene to go Christmas shopping like I promised. We walk to the town square for a little exercise, despite the frigid air. It is quite literally the Christmas capital—like on a North Pole level. Garlands stuffed with thick red poinsettias wind around every lamppost. Silver bells hang off the signs on every street corner. Like in the song. There are probably sixteen or so places of business, and they each have decorated storefronts.

"Tell me you're obsessed with Christmas without telling me you're obsessed with Christmas," I say.

"Isn't it so cute?" Sharlene asks.

"There's gotta be a hidden camera somewhere." I peer around Sharlene. "Be honest, we're on a show called *Christmas Gone Wild*."

Sharlene bumps my arm. "Come on, Rose. Admit it.

It's starting to grow on you."

I roll my eyes and shrug.

"I made a list of all the people I need to shop for." She pulls out her phone and opens her Notes app. "What do you think about getting a gift for Ms. Flores?"

"That's a nice idea. And it would be nice to do something to put a smile on her face. Seems like she's going through a lot with the trees and trying to sell a place that's been home to her for so long," Sharlene says.

I nod. "I can't imagine having to sell it after it's been a big part of her life. I mean, it's her husband's legacy."

"Okay, so I'm moving her to the top of the list." She looks up at me and smirks. "So what about you and Malcolm?"

I let out a frustrated breath. "There is no *me and Malcolm*."

"There used to be," she shoots back.

We walk past a few stores, and I pull my scarf up higher to stave off the icy air. "That was a long time ago. We're different people now."

"Uh-uh. I saw the two of you at the main house. There's something there. And maybe it's a mix of something that never died and something new. Two things can be true."

"We were talking about plant fungicide," I deadpan.

Sharlene smirks. "Looked pretty cozy to me—no

matter the subject matter."

"If we did, it's because we're just friends. There's a familiarity there. Malcolm never could be clear about his feelings, but I got his message once he ended things before culinary school." I open the door to one of the quaint shops, Arabella's Gift Shop, and head inside. It smells like pine and mountain air. It even smells like Christmas everywhere in this town.

Sharlene pulls her scarf down so it's no longer covering her face and drapes loosely around her neck. "That was a long time ago. And his mom had just died."

I spin around so I can look at her. "And he couldn't be bothered to pick up the phone once? He meant everything to me. I wanted to be there for him, and he wouldn't let me."

Sharlene lets out a deep breath. "That's valid. I'm just asking you to look at things through a different lens. Maybe it wasn't about you. And now that I've seen you two together after nine years have passed, I think you need to give it another shot."

I shake my head. I refuse to entertain a second chance. Sometimes we don't get them. "We missed our shot when the buzzer sounded, which means game over."

Sharlene is looking at a reindeer mug, which she sets down. She stares me down. "There's always another chance for a team victory, even if it's another season."

That one catches me off guard. I don't have a response for it, so I just smile. "Are we gonna talk about Malcolm Sharpe all day, or are we going to do some shopping?"

Sharlene's eyes shine. "Both."

"You win the Most Irksome Sister Award." I press my lips together and give her a side-eye.

She laughs and shrugs her shoulders. "I kind of like that title."

I keep asking myself what I'm doing as I walk toward Malcolm's bakery. When he challenged me earlier, I got caught up in our old ways. We used to be playfully competitive, and it almost felt like second nature to accept his challenge. But now that I'm alone with my thoughts, they all settle enough for me to see just one, slowly rising from the dust to the top of my mind: It's just going to be me and Malcolm. Me *alone* with Malcolm.

When I arrive to the front of his shop, he's fiddling with a string of Christmas lights in the window. It takes him a second before he sees me, and I study the way his muscles flex under his fitted sweater sleeves. The way his eyebrows crease when the string slips out of his hand. The way his face scrunches when he continues to fight with it so it stays put. *Butterflies, butterflies, butterflies.* He notices me then and waves, his eyes glowing from the lights he's standing in front of. I wave back. For a few beats, we stare at each other, a complete reflection. And then the door unlocks and swings open.

Ralph holds it open, a sly smile on his face. "What's up, Rose. You coming in?"

I snap my head in his direction. "Uh, yeah." I make my way over to the door and enter while Ralph holds it open for me. "Thanks," I tell him.

Malcolm steps away from the window. "Welcome."

My head swivels to look at everything. The glass display once full of treats is now empty, the glass perfectly polished. There's still the scent of sweetness from the oven, though. I imagine there's always something to bake.

"My first visit here was a little...surprising. But this really is such a beautiful place," I say.

Ralph holds both hands out at his sides. "Where baking magic happens."

Malcolm laughs. "Everything all good for today?" he asks Ralph.

"Yeah. Distribution execs called again today, though." His smile fades, and his expression twists into something more serious.

Malcolm drops his smile too. "I know, I know."

That must be the distributors he mentioned when he mentioned the deal. He still hasn't called them back?

He's running. He does this when he's scared of change—purposely do the opposite of what he should so whatever good thing he has is ruined. Then he doesn't have to make the choice himself. It's made for him.

"Patience is running thin." Ralph presses his lips together.

Malcolm sighs, his body slouching. "I'll make sure I call by tomorrow."

Ralph reaches for his coat and pulls it on. "Don't think I need to say more, then. I just texted Sharlene, and we're going to go grab dinner up at the main house. You two have a good night."

Sharlene? Going to have to ask her about that later. I didn't even realize they'd exchanged numbers.

I take my coat off and sling it over one of the chairs. "You too, Ralph."

"Night, Ralph," Malcolm says. Ralph nods on his way out, the bells on the door jingling to signal his departure. "Ready to head back?" he asks me.

"Yeah," I say.

He holds the swing door open for me by leaning his back against it, and I try—Lord, I try—my hardest not to touch him. The universe has other plans, though, because of course my chest grazes against his. Is this not a standard doorway? Because it feels smaller. It's a brief touch, but it doesn't stop the crackling sparks from slipping down my spine. For the duration of the touch, our eyes meet, but I look away before it can turn into something else.

Malcolm clears his throat. "I, uh, have aprons here so you don't get flour all over your clothes." He reaches behind the door and pulls two off the rack while I lean against the stainless steel island.

There's my old Malcolm, always thinking ahead for me. He slips the solid black one around his head and then holds up one that's red with a gingerbread pattern. "May I?" he asks.

I nod my head before thoughts even have the chance to form. He takes a step and places the loop over my head, his fingers grazing over my collarbone, triggering goosebumps across my whole body. He maintains eye contact as his hands travel down both sides of the apron until they reach the strings. Meanwhile, my heart starts a revolution in my chest, possibly on the verge of crashing through my ribcage. As we stay facing each other, his arms extend around me to tie the strings together at my back. He's in my space, taking his time while he ties a bow. My breath catches in my throat, and I'm certain my body just forgot how breathing works—forgot that it needs to breathe to stay alive.

When he finishes tying the bow, he doesn't move away, just keeps his hands still in the final stage tying a bow requires. I look into what used to be my favorite set of eyes, and for a few moments, all the time between when he left and now disappears. He studies me, and his eyes go on a world tour around my face, ending at my lips. When I feel something rebuilding between us, I take a step back. He can't just reopen my heart for business when he's the one who closed it.

I swallow. "Maybe we should get started. It's, um... getting late, and I don't want Sharlene to wonder where I am." That part is true. It's supposed to be a sister trip, after all. Then again, Sharlene is the one who got me into this mess.

"Yeah," he says, taking a step back too and dropping his hands to his sides. I try not to read into it, but he looks...disappointed? It only lasts for a second, though, because he straightens then flashes me a slick smile. "You ready to lose?"

I shake my head. "I don't lose." I keep my voice collected and confident. Gran's recipe has never failed me, and it isn't about to now.

He laughs as he starts pulling ingredients out of cabinets and the fridge.

I bite my bottom lip and hesitate then decide to ask, "So, the distribution execs Ralph mentioned...were those the same ones who have to do with the deal you mentioned?"

"The very ones," he says.

"Any clarity on that since we last talked?"

He drops a box of raisins on the counter and pauses. "It's not that I don't want to do it, but it requires some travel, and I'll be busier. I'm worried about being away from the bakery and Ms. Flores. I honestly don't know if I can balance the time."

"You have Ralph, right? Can't he step in to help when you're not around?"

He empties the box of raisins in a glass bowl. "That covers the bakery, but what about Ms. Flores? I live at the tree farm's lodge, and I work nearby. I can usually drop anything I'm doing if she needs me. What if she needs me when I'm on the road?"

"She probably won't need much help when the tree farm is sold, right?" He pauses for a moment, and his shoulders tense.

"That's true," he says.

"Your shoulders just got all tense. What's wrong?" I ask.

He lets out a long breath. "She's older, you know. And she's only going to keep getting older. What if I'm not..." He can't bring himself to finish the sentence.

And now I get it. What if something happens and he's not there? Just like with his mom. "Oh, Malcolm." I reach across the table and cover his hand with mine. "Your mom's accident didn't happen because you weren't there. It happened because life just sucks sometimes."

He swallows, his watery eyes fixed on me. "I should have been there. I tried to make it back, but I was too late. She was just...gone. I can't go through that again. I need to stay close."

I squeeze his hand. "She knows, Malcolm. She knows you would have been there if you could. And knowing Ms. Sharpe, I don't think she would have wanted you to carry this. And I think I know what she'd say about that distribution deal too."

"What?" he asks.

"She'd want you to take it if that was your dream. Your mom is the one who taught you to bake. She knew what she was doing. She saw the possibilities before you did. If you truly don't think the distribution deal is a good fit, then don't take it. But if it's what you want, then you'd be wasting your mother's efforts if you don't."

He blinks a few times. "I never thought about it like that."

"Yeah, sometimes we don't see all the angles when we're sad."

He nods. "You know, you could do the same thing. Maybe it's time to start looking at things from a different angle. You were so good with the trees, despite them not being your specialty. Maybe it's time for you to expand too, just in a different way."

"But I can't even land a new client," I say. The words are bitter on my tongue.

"You don't need new clients, Rose. You just need to be open to new things. You just need *you*."

I take a minute to think through what he just said. This trip was supposed to be a way for me to clear my thoughts, but instead, they're all jumbled and indistinguishable. Maybe Malcolm is right. Maybe I do need to start looking at things from a different angle. I'm not sure what that means yet, but I know it means *something*.

I look up at him and smile. "Okay, Mr. Sugar Cakes. Enough talking. I need to bake my winning sweet bread." I crack my knuckles, stretch my arms up to the ceiling, and roll my neck. He stares back at me with an amused expression, so I pick up the rolling pin and point it at him. "Now, don't try to steal my recipe."

"I'm not worried. I have home court advantage." He pops a raisin in his mouth.

"Weren't we just talking about new angles? Time for some of that new perspective. Something fresh and exciting," I say.

"Exciting, indeed," he says, his eyes on me. They shouldn't, but the words make me tingle, my body turning into a human sparkler.

For the next hour and a half, we work on our respective recipes on opposite ends of the table. Malcolm turns on Christmas music, which fills the silence, and he hums along to familiar melodies. Ordinarily, I'd be sick from a mini Christmas concert like this, but hearing the low rumble of his voice alongside the songs feels like some kind of warm comfort. Every now and then, we bump into each other or reach for the same ingredient. But overall, we fall into a rhythm, and we're able to bake our sweet breads.

Just as I'm stirring my mixture, Kelly Clarkson's "Every Christmas" rings through the kitchen. I realize that I could use some more raisins. But when I reach for the bowl, Malcolm grabs my hand, pulls me away from the counter, and twirls me twice. At the second twirl, he pulls me in so I'm flush against his chest, my heart rate skyrocketing. I laugh as he sways me back and forth a few times before letting me go again. It's like he knows I'll get skittish if he holds on too long. He's right. But I'm also afraid of the reason I would.

While we finish baking, he tells me funny stories about his time here in Holly Oaks. As we chat, I remember how much I loved talking to him, and an ache I thought I'd thrown into the abyss comes tumbling back. This is exactly what I've spent nine years trying to avoid. I should have been able to close that client. I should be back home in Orlando, working on integrating them into our existing workload. I shouldn't be in Holly Oaks, baking sweet bread and trading jokes with Malcolm Sharpe. I darn sure shouldn't be dancing pressed against him in his kitchen. And my heart certainly shouldn't be tripping over every glance he throws my way. It's the first time I think it: That trouble I wasn't looking for? It just might have found me.

Nine

It's no surprise that, to the people of Holly Oaks, the sweet bread competition is very serious business. When Sharlene and I enter the main lodge, it seems like the whole town is gathered in the common area. Pockets of people laugh and socialize with each other while they drink every kind of holiday drink imaginable. Eggnog, hot chocolate, cider, gingerbread tea, pumpkin spice fill-in-the-blank. "Baby Please Come Home" plays softly in the background, everyone glowing from the Christmas lights around the whole main house.

I spot Ralph near the cider and remember our last encounter.

I lean closer to Sharlene and say, "I didn't know you

and Ralph were getting so close."

A smile plays at her lips. "We're just getting to know each other. He's here. I'm here."

"Mm-hmm," I say.

"Oh, please. I can admit I'm attracted to him, unlike you and—"

"Shar," I warn.

She cackles, and I give her a sharp look.

Across the room—and because we just know how to always find each other—I catch Malcolm's eye. He's chatting in a group of people along with Ms. Flores. But when he sees me, he stops mid-sip and smiles. And then it's just me and him. All those holiday drinks, all the chatter, all the Christmas music and lights—gone. I feel another one of my do-it-yourself stitches come undone, and it scares me how everything inside of me feels like it's on a warmer, all my cold fading away.

Sharlene leans in and snaps me out of my trance. "I'm going to get us some cider. I could use something warm after the walk here." She pauses and smirks. "Although, I see you've already found something warm."

I roll my eyes. "You know, the Irksome Sister Award is already yours. No need to keep proving yourself."

She pats my shoulder. "Nah, just trying to keep the title now."

I shake my head as she hurries off.

I look over to Malcolm again, and he's making his way to me, so I move in his direction too.

When we meet in the middle, he says, "You look beautiful."

I fiddle with one of my curls, suddenly self-conscious. I don't know why he says it. I'm wearing winter clothes, and my hair is wind-blown and probably forming tiny icicles. "Um, thanks."

He beams. "So, you ready?"

I raise an eyebrow. "To win? Absolutely."

He chuckles. "So confident all the time. Some things never change, huh."

I shrug.

"I meant, are you ready to admit that I'm the best sweet bread baker in all the land?" He lifts his chin.

"Ha!" I say. "Not possible. Gran's recipe won't fail me."

Mayor Gregory taps the mic. She's dressed down today in a sparkly red cardigan and jeans. The strands of her bob peek out from a matching sparkly Santa hat. "Welcome to the annual Holly Oaks Sweet Bread Contest. We're so glad you all could make it out tonight. As always, a huge thank you to Malcolm Sharpe, who started a contest we didn't know we needed."

Everyone around the room cheers. Some people lift their glasses.

Mayor Gregory moves to stand in front of a long oak

table with three people. "Let's give it up for our judges. Mr. Roman of Roman's Diner, Mrs. Jones from Off the Rack Bike Shop, and Miss Delilah from Smoothie Queen!"

More claps, cheers, and hooting. Again, I think: *Christmas Gone Wild*.

"May we have the blindfolds, please?" Mayor Gregory asks. One of the volunteers, a sweet teenager with reindeer glasses, begins tying the blindfolds on the three judges.

Mayor Gregory whispers a thank you to the girl then faces the crowd again. "Let's bring out the sweet bread!"

The same volunteer enters the room again, arms square and holding a large tray of sweet bread slices. They are organized in five rows, each with three plates and an identifying number. I'm lured away from the moment when my phone vibrates in my pocket. I pull it out, glance down at it, and realize it's a 407 number I don't recognize. It's for sure an Orlando number, but I'm busy now, so I push the button to stop it from vibrating and shove it back in my pocket.

As the judges taste samples, people whisper to each other, speculating as to who each one belongs to. I'm slightly nervous because I do want to win, but I'd never admit that to Malcolm. Occasionally, he glances over at me, the smug expression never leaving his eyes. Once all the judges finish their tasting, they chat with each other for a few moments before nodding their heads in agreement. Miss Delilah from the Smoothie Queen signals to Mayor Gregory. When she whispers the winner in her ear, Mayor Gregory nods then checks her clipboard to see who's attached to the number.

For a second, I panic at the way a slow smile spreads across her lips. It makes me think she knew this person would win. And if Malcolm wins every year, then that slow smile might be for someone familiar. My stomach sinks when I think about how he'll gloat until the end of time.

Mayor Gregory clears her throat. "And we have a winner by unanimous vote." Her smile gets wider.

Unanimous. God, he really did win.

Malcolm leans in then, his lips inches from my ear. I hate that my body betrays me by reacting to it. Something warm sizzles down my spine.

"Time to get my crown," he says.

"We'll see," I shoot back.

Mayor Gregory pauses for dramatic effect then says, "Congratulations, Rose Douglas. You are this year's Holly Oaks Sweet Bread Champion!"

The room erupts in applause, and I squeal then jump, lifting both my hands in the air. Sharlene wraps both her arms around my waist and squeezes. Warmth rises in my heart like a high tide. I only catch a glimpse of Malcolm, and he looks...proud? Before I can process it, I'm whisked away by random people in the crowd pushing me forward.

"Don't be shy, come and get your trophy," Mayor Gregory calls.

Once I'm up front, Mayor Gregory rams the trophy in my hands, and immediately, a group of people I don't know gather around me. It's only a few seconds before the mayor is slipping an arm around my shoulder and posing us for photos. It makes me giddy but exhausted all at once.

I let it go on for a few more minutes before excusing myself, pulling on my coat, and sneaking out to the back deck that overlooks the Christmas tree. I stare out at it, seeing it in a way that I hadn't the night it was lit. Looking at it now, it's magical against the sparkly night sky and the mountains in the distance. Did I just think the word *magical*? I'm clearly spending too much time here. All this Christmas is getting to my head.

"I guess congratulations are in order." I don't even need to turn around to recognize that low, gravelly, confident voice. It's one branded on my mind and heart.

Malcolm joins me at the banister I'm leaning on.

I smile at him and look back out at the tree. "Thanks for encouraging me to do it. I had a lot of fun."

"No prob." He lets out a small laugh. "Although, I didn't expect you to usurp my title."

I throw my head back and laugh too. "It's hard to beat Gran's recipe."

His arm moves, and a sliver of it brushes against mine. "True."

For a while we sit in a comfortable quiet, then he says, "I stopped celebrating Christmas when I left. Mom loved it so much, and I'd see her in everything—ornaments, Christmas lights, poinsettias. And it all made me so sad. But then I came here. This town and Ms. Flores all made me realize I don't want to spend my life with my memories of her stuffed in some dark corner of my mind. That would mean forgetting her. I don't want that. I want to remember her and her love of Christmas. I want to keep feeling close to her."

There's a heaviness in my chest when I think of him feeling sad. "I think that would make her happy."

He nods.

I look at him from the corner of my eye. "I have a confession."

He turns to face me, one arm still leaning on the banister. "What's that?"

I try not to smile, but the corner of my mouth ticks up. "I have to admit, this tree really is beautiful. And I don't know what it is, but there's some kind of magic energy. I felt it as soon as I stepped out here."

"That's what we've been trying to tell you." He

gestures around him.

"I might even do something wild. Like decorate one. I'm trying everything else, and you know what they say, *when in Holly Oaks...*" I shrug.

"Hold on. Are you telling me that you've never decorated a Christmas tree?" He blinks several times. "Because you can't be serious."

My mouth pinches to a straight line. "You know my parents weren't big on Christmas decorations. We did the gifts, and that was it."

"I mean, I remember you saying that, but I guess it didn't register that you didn't have a tree." He shakes his head. "What a shame. You know how much effort goes into picking out the perfect tree?"

I furrow my brows. "I wouldn't know. I guess we were always taught, *what's the point of putting up decorations you just have to take down anyway?*"

Malcolm gasps and places a hand on his chest like I just told him he only had a day to live. "Are you kidding me? The decorating is the best part. You hang ornaments and lights, and the fire is going, and there's Christmas music and family bonding."

"I guess I just never had time for it. I put everything I have into Plant Ladies. I can't afford to spend time decorating when I could be marketing, or emailing, or taking meetings with potential clients."

"Mmm." Malcom switches his position so he's back facing the trees. "It's one of the reasons I decided to move to Holly Oaks in the first place. We have our busy moments, but everyone makes time to slow down to do things like go to the bakeoff and decorate the Christmas tree. It's a different life here."

"It feels like a dreamland, but I think I might like slowing down." I think of my phone ringing earlier and how I didn't bother to pick it up. If I were back home, I would have immediately swiped right to answer. What is happening to me?

"It looks good on you," Malcolm says.

Our gazes connect. He studies me, and once more, I see something flicker over his face—something I can't quite make out. But the door opens, jolting both of us out of the moment.

"Malcolm, Rose! Come inside." Ms. Flores gestures with her hands, her petite frame like a shadow against the warm glow of the room behind her. "We need to get a picture of all the competitors and, of course, our winner." She hurries back inside, letting the door shut behind her.

Malcolm tucks a loose strand of my hair behind my ear. "Your fans await."

I don't know what to do with that, so I nod and make my way inside.

Ten

Serial killer. It's the first place my brain goes when a tap on my window startles me out of sleep. Holly Oaks is the perfect stage for it. I knew this place was too remote. Anyone can get away with anything here because everyone here looks at the world through Christmas-colored glasses. I rub my eyes, and there's a piece of paper taped to the window.

The tapping happens again. I groan and drag myself out of bed. Does no one want me to get sleep on this vacation? When I get close enough to read the note, it says:

Early Christmas present at the front door.

For me? I open the window and look around, but it's

just trees, snow, and mountains. I shut it then pull on my fuzzy robe over my pajamas and head for the front door. The icy air pushes against my face when I open the door. I look both ways, and to the left is a Christmas tree leaning against the wall with another note.

For Rose

Love,

Your secret admirer

Tucking the note under my arm, I struggle a bit but manage to drag the tree inside then lean it against the interior wall near the door. It only takes me a minute before I remember my conversation with Malcolm about never decorating a tree. Something takes flight in me as I replay that and picture him walking through the rows of trees on the west end of the tree farm, taking his time to pick out a tree just right for me. I reach for the note under my arm and read it again. The word love whirlwinds through my brain, stirring the memory of the first time I thought he might love me. We had just gone out for karaoke for a friend's birthday. I belted out the lyrics to Mary J. Blige's "No One Will Do" until my lungs hurt, my eyes on him the entire song. When I slid into the booth next to him in the dim light of the restaurant, he leaned in and said, "I only want you too."

My heart squeezes in my chest no matter how much I try to make it stop. The more time I spend in Holly

Oaks, the harder it is to keep resisting whatever is going on inside me.

The creak of Sharlene's room door pushes my thoughts away. "Morning," she says, rubbing her eyes.

"Oh, you're tired? Sounds familiar," I say.

She gives me a little chuckle. "All the town activities have really worn me out. I mean, I'm having fun, but these folks go hard for Christmas." She eyes the tree by the door, and they perk up like she's just been given a shot of holiday espresso. "Speaking of which, did you get a tree?"

I roll my eyes and hand her the note.

Her lips expand to a full-blown smile as she reads. "As if it wasn't obvious who the admirer would be." She smirks.

"Don't start. You haven't even had breakfast yet."

"Fine. I'll eat my Wheaties first, and then I'll start my musings about your note." She laughs and enters the kitchen. "Want some hot chocolate?"

I nod. "I'm not sure I'll ever get sick of it. It's out of this world."

"Agreed," Sharlene says, unscrewing the lid on the thermos we brought back from the main lodge last night. "Also, I was right. Everything in Holly Oaks is just as amazing as I said."

I shake my head. "You just had to slip that in

there, huh? You know you're not always right about everything, right?"

Her smile grows ten sizes. "But this time I am. And I have a feeling it's going to pay off."

I narrow my eyes at her. I'm about to ask her what she means, but there's a knock on the door. I look at Sharlene, and she shrugs.

When I open the door, Malcolm and Ms. Flores smile back at me.

"I hope you don't mind us dropping by," Ms. Flores says.

I try to ignore the pandemonium my heart causes when my eyes connect with Malcolm's.

"Uh, no. I mean, yeah." *Get it together, Rose You're embarrassing yourself.* "Please, come in." I step aside and open the door wider.

I catch Malcolm's faint citrusy-cedar scent as he walks past me and have to fight the urge to close my eyes.

Malcolm smiles and waves at Sharlene, who waves back then faces me. "The plant medicine is here."

"That was fast," Sharlene says from the kitchen.

"Oh," I say. I don't mean it to come out disappointed, but it does.

Ms. Flores places a hand on my arm. "It's a good thing, dear."

I try to smile, but I know it's weak. "I'm sorry. I didn't mean it like that. It's just that I know how much this place means to you, and I don't want to disappoint you." And then it clicks. It's not just Ms. Flores that I'm worried about disappointing. I don't want to disappoint *him* either.

Ms. Flores chuckles. "I know this isn't foolproof. And besides, you wouldn't be disappointing me. It's the plant food that would be the disappointment." She winks. "Besides, there's always a chance for a sprinkle of magic."

"Amen," Sharlene says.

She's really holding strong to that magical trees theory. "I know how much this place means, and I'd hate for something to ruin the sale."

"We're just glad you gave us a fighting chance, Rose. Seriously," Malcolm says. He's looking at me with so much sincerity I almost want to run to him and wrap my arms around him.

Ms. Flores's buttery smile falters a little. "Besides, that buyer we mentioned seems like they may be the only candidate."

"Oh?" Sharlene says, stepping out of the kitchen. "Did they agree to honor the legacy of the farm and all the traditions?"

Ms. Flores swallows then sighs. "Well, they didn't quite say it in so many words. They think the traditions are great, but they also think there's an opportunity to expand them to attract more visitors."

I scrunch my face. "More visitors? I hope I'm not overstepping, but doesn't that seem like they're more financially motivated, rather than community focused?" A few days ago, I couldn't care less about the Holly Oaks Tree Farm, but now that I've spent time here, I don't want to see it sold off to someone who isn't going to keep its legacy going. It's not just a tree farm. It's a place for community and family and joy.

Ms. Flores studies me for a few beats, like she's trying to work her thoughts out. But then she shakes her head. "At least they'll consider keeping some things the same." She pauses and looks at the floor. "I wish I could do better. I just want everything my Francisco started to continue."

Malcolm squeezes her shoulder. "He knows you're doing the best you can."

Ms. Flores's eyes go glassy. "You know he took such a risk when he bought this place. There were no traditions, of course. But he started by slowly involving the town, then added more and more with every passing year. He took a plain tree farm and made it a home for the whole town. His entire heart is in this place."

"A risk, huh," Malcolm whispers. He glances at me but looks away.

Okay.

A tiny laugh escapes Ms. Flores. "He always projected

confidence, but he didn't have a clue what he was doing. This tree farm could have failed, and he was just as afraid as anyone else would have been."

Malcolm blinks. "Did he ever tell you how he pushed past all that fear?"

She nods. "He had come across a quote that put things in perspective. It was about *never knowing being more painful than taking the risk and failing.*"

Again, Malcolm blinks, probably thinking about his own lack of risk with the bakery and its distribution deal.

Ms. Flores pats his arm. "Sometimes, you just have to jump. No wondering if you're ready, or if it's going to work out. You can find that out later. But you won't know unless you jump."

He sighs. "You mean the execs and the bakery."

"I think you know I mean more than just the bakery." She smirks and throws me a glance so brief I second-guess if it happened.

Malcolm locks his jaw. "Ms. Flores."

She holds both hands up. "All I'm saying is that second chances don't always come 'round."

Malcolm rubs the side of his jaw, which remains tight. He nods, a secret language of some sort between them.

"Now, you mess around, and you might not even get a second chance with those execs. It's your time right now."

"Yes, ma'am." Malcolm salutes her and smiles.

She taps his arm. "We better get going. I don't want to waste another second. We've got to at least try. Right, Rose?"

I nod, despite the chaos and disorder in my stomach.

Hours later, after spraying trees, bending down to examine them, and walking endless rows, we're finally done. Ms. Flores is really lucky it's a controlled area and that she has help.

I think of my gran and what she would do, so I lean over and whisper, "Don't worry, the medicine is going to make things better. It's just a matter of time before you're well again."

"You really think the talking will help?" Malcolm's deep voice hangs in the quietness.

I jump then put a hand on my chest. "Don't scare me like that." My voice is breathless and unsteady.

He laughs, and it echoes through me, a rhythm of warmth repeated again and again.

"Some things never change," he says.

He's referring to how easy it was to sneak up and scare me when we were younger.

"It's not funny." I lightly push his shoulder. "And yeah, I do think talking to them helps. As you know, Gran had a flourishing garden in her front yard. She talked to her plants every day. That was her secret."

"And she always had a plant sitter if she had to leave town. Talking probably works better than that fancy plant medicine, I bet."

"I know so. But I think we'll play it safe." I lift the pressurized sprayer containing the plant food. "Hopefully, the chlorothalonil in here will help."

Malcolm wrinkles his brows. "Cloro—what? Sounds...intense."

The two of us look at each other and burst into laughter. I love laughing with him. I feel a pull in my heart again for the time period when we were us. It's the first time I admit to myself that I miss him. I shake the thought free, and when I blink it away, I notice him staring at me.

"What?" I ask. My cheeks heat under his gaze, a thing that's familiar and foreign all at once.

He shakes his head. "Nothing."

It doesn't feel like nothing. I decide to change the subject anyway. "You know, a strange thing happened this morning." I run a hand along the branches of one of the trees.

"Oh yeah? What's that?"

It appears the Christmas Fairy visited my cabin and left a gift. Would you know anything about that?"

Malcolm smirks. "Really? They've been known to frequent places like Holly Oaks. Like we've been trying to tell you: magic is all around. What did they leave you?"

My head whips in his direction. "Like you don't know."

He shrugs and presses his lips tight.

"Fine. I'll play along. Looks like I have a tree to decorate." I turn back to the tree in front of me and hold a branch in my palm to inspect it.

"Funny how that all worked out for you, considering you've never decorated a tree."

I glance back at him, and again, my stomach flips, refusing order. I hesitate, but ultimately decide to take a risk. "You wouldn't happen to know where I could find some ornaments, would you?"

He pretends to think hard, rubbing his chin back and forth. "I might."

"If you might know where to find them, do you think you might consider bringing them by my cabin? Since it's my first time decorating and all."

All he does now is look at me. No smile. Just his deep amber eyes.

I panic for a few seconds. He doesn't have time. And how presumptuous of me to think he wants to spend time decorating a tree with me when that would require...well, his time. That's what I get for taking risks. "If you're too busy..."

But he stops me mid-sentence when his hand traces my jawline. His glove is on, but I feel the trail of warmth his hand leaves anyway. "I'm never too busy for you. I'll be there—with ornaments on."

I'm in high school again—at least that's what it feels like every time I try to steer my brain away from the very winding path of Malcolm Sharpe. It's futile, though, because I find my thoughts drifting to him like they're on autopilot, and once Sharlene leaves the cabin to help Ms. Flores plan the annual Christmas Eve party, I try on a million sweaters. Then, after I do that, I fiddle with my curls for an obscene amount of time. I flop down on the couch to wait for him to arrive and groan. I've already allowed my thoughts to drift to him far too many times already while I'm alone. How many times must I remind my brain of this before it's convinced? Malcolm Sharpe hurt me once, and if I let too many of my feelings out of their box, he might hurt me again. He'll have all the power again after I've fought so hard to get it back. Besides, Holly Oaks is his home. I'm just a visitor. We'd never work anyway.

A knock on the door stops my spiraling thoughts. I open the door, and when I see those starry brown eyes peering back at me, that confection smile that fills me with warm comfort, I don't remember a single thing I was just thinking about.

"So, can I come in?" Malcolm raises an eyebrow.

"Right. Su—sure." I step aside, mentally scolding myself for not only staring but bumbling over my words.

"Thanks." He takes a step inside.

It's then that I look down and notice he's pulling a wagon full of Christmas decorations: Bright-colored ornaments, lush garland, bundles of Christmas lights.

I blink, my mouth half open as I study the wagon. "Wow, that's a lot of Christmas."

He chortles. "And what isn't in Holly Oaks?"

"Fair point. I suppose I should have known that by now."

"You're failing your Christmas 101 test, Rose."

I laugh. "So where did all of this come from?"

He places the wagon near a fairly empty spot in the corner. "We have a lot of decorations that have accumulated over the years. Plus, Ms. Flores likes variety."

Of course she does. The whole town apparently likes variety—as long as it's specifically of the Christmas variety. No other holidays permitted. Malcolm unzips his coat and pulls it off. I catch sight of the way his top half fills out his fitted sweater. My eyes travel the curve of his neck to his broad shoulders and chest, the muscles on his arm hugged tightly by the sweater sleeves. I swallow.

He clears his throat, totally catching me.

Oh my God.

Before he can call me on it. I grab the coat from his hands. "I'll, um...hang this up for you." The words come out fast, and I also make sure I move away from him with the same energy. I don't look at him either, because it will only scramble my brain more.

He chuckles and reaches for a container at the top of the wagon. When I turn around from hanging his coat on the hook by the door, he's facing me on the other side of the room. "I brought you something." He shakes the container he's holding.

"Oh yeah?" I ask, taking a few cautious steps toward him. I'm so afraid to get close, since my brain and my body forget their jobs when he's around.

He meets me halfway and hands me the container. I narrow my eyes as he passes it to me.

"Don't worry, it's not Christmas elixir," he says.

I feel the corner of my mouth tick up, another body part betraying me. I make a dramatic show of lifting the lid, and when I do, I gasp. I look up at him, eyes wide. The loaf of neatly sliced black cake sits in the container. I close my eyes and inhale the sweet, fruity scent.

When his lips curl into a smile, I physically feel my heart open in invitation.

"You baked this for me?"

"Yeah, I did," he says, rubbing the back of his neck.

"Didn't think you remembered," I say.

"I remember everything about you."

My eyes dart up to meet his. For a moment, we just stand there. I would expect it to feel awkward. Two people with all this tense history between them. But it's the opposite. It feels like a moment I can fit into. A moment that's better than comfort itself.

Finally, my brain wakes up, and I interrupt our haze. "Thank you. I know this cake is a lot of work..."

"Worth it," he says.

"This is gonna be our reward for finishing the tree," I say.

"And you're willing to share with me?" His lips break into a wicked smile.

The way he says that word...share. Like he's not just talking about the cake. Nope. I'm not going to think about what he meant. I'm good.

I just nod at him and set it down on the coffee table. "We should probably get started."

He looks around. "So where's Sharlene?"

"She was all excited because Ms. Flores asked her to help with the Christmas Eve party planning up at the main house."

"Ah, yes, her famous Christmas Eve party." Malcolm eyes the fire. "I see your Girl Scout skills have developed."

I shrug. "Figured I better learn since we'll be here a while. Didn't think you'd want me calling you every second to build a fire."

"I would have." He pauses. "And can we get something straight?"

I pretend to look through the decorations in the wagon. Anything to not have to meet his eyes. "Of course." I stuff the words with as much nonchalance as I can.

"I know it's been a while for us. But I don't want you thinking you can't call on me for things. I'm here for whatever you need while you're in Holly Oaks, okay?"

I do look at him then. I want him to pull me close, let me rest my head on his shoulder while I listen to the rhythm of his heart. Instead, I keep my feelings folded neatly and say, "Okay."

"Good." He covers my hand with his to stop me from picking up an ornament. "We gotta do the lights first."

"Right. Lights." I let out a breath, still not over the contact.

"So, what have I missed in Orlando?" he asks, untangling a bundle of lights.

I pick up my own bundle to untangle and scrunch my face. "Not much. They did get rid of the old Orlando Lanes Bowling Alley, though."

"Nooooo," he says with a low grimace.

I nod.

"That was the spot back in the day." He pauses, unwinding part of the string. "And what about you? You, uh, dating anyone?" He doesn't meet my gaze, just keeps fiddling with the string of lights.

My insides freeze up at the question. I swallow. "I'm not. Plant Ladies keeps me pretty busy, so I haven't really had much time to date."

He lets out an audible breath.

"And you?" The question is quiet and not as composed as I intend.

"Nah. Same. Between the bakery and helping Ms. Flores, I can't really be there for someone the way I'd want to."

Kind of like he couldn't have been there for me when we split. At least he's honest.

For the next hour, we string lights and hang ornaments while Christmas songs like "I'll be Home for Christmas" play in the background. We work in sync and sneak pieces of black cake, even though we both agreed we'd save it to the end.

I grab the last ornament and scan the tree for an empty spot. There's one up top, so I stand on the tips of my toes for the branch, but it's just out of reach. Malcolm is behind me in a swift second, his fingers faint on my hip, the light press of his chest against my back.

He stretches up with his free hand to take the ornament from me and place it on the tree. My cheeks heat along with the rest of my body from his proximity. I'm almost afraid to, but I chance a glance back at him. His eyes darken under the hood of those thick lashes. If we were the us of nine years ago, I'd spin myself to face him, throw my arms around his neck, and press my lips to his.

I can't let myself go there again, so I slip past him instead and step back to admire our work. My heart feels full of Christmas and joy...and *love*.

"You want to do the honors?" Malcolm asks, handing me the cords for the tree.

"Maybe you should," I say.

"No way. It's a first for you." He juts his chin at me. "Go ahead."

I connect the two cords, and the tree lights up. It's nowhere near the size of the tree at the lighting the other night, but somehow, it's more magical.

"Wow," I say.

Malcolm turns his head toward me. "Yeah, wow."

I blush when my focus shifts to him, and his eyes are on me, not the tree. He's making it so hard for me to continue my resistance.

"I'm glad you like the tree, Rose. And I'm really glad you asked me to share this with you."

I smile. "I should be thanking you—for the tree and

the Christmas experience."

"It was only fair I do something nice for you too. You're the one making all the miracles happen."

"Me? Nah. I just offered a potential solution. Nothing's set yet."

"It's a better shot than we had before. Seriously, we're all grateful for your help. You're out here inspiring trees and business moves." He chuckles.

I give him a puzzled look.

"I'm taking the risk. Meeting with the distributors tomorrow."

I squeal, throwing myself into his arms without thinking—the exact opposite of what my brain just told me a second ago to *not* do. When his hands find my waist and his fingers dig into my hips, I jump back. My instinct tells me to apologize, but I don't. Because the truth is, I'm not sorry.

"I'm really proud of you," I tell him.

He's still processing the closeness of our bodies and, I assume, the way I practically sprinted out of his arms. But he just smiles and says, "Couldn't have done it without you."

Eleven

Sharlene allows me to sleep in the following morning as a reward for spilling the beans about my evening with Malcolm. I'm grateful for the time alone with myself. I lie in bed for hours, trying to work out my feelings. There are moments from before, when Malcolm and I were us, that keep rising, rising, rising. And I don't know what to do with them. Do I let him in again? Do I let him hold this fragile, heart-shaped thing that keeps me alive when clarity fell short back then and might again? I'm not sure it can survive another fall.

After the morning to myself, Sharlene and I grab lunch in the main house. When we enter the dining room, Ms. Flores is sitting at a table with a sandwich in front of her. Sharlene and I make our way over to her.

"Hey, Ms. Flores," I say.

"Sharlene, Rose. How are you doing?" She points the other chairs at the table.

I pull out a chair and sit. "Merry." I cover my mouth with my hand. It's out before I even have a chance to think it through, like some kind of reflex.

Ms. Flores and Sharlene both dart their heads in my direction. I'm afraid to look at them, but when I do, their eyes are wide and bright, like they've been stuffed with Christmas lights.

Ms. Flores smirks. "Merry, huh. Could it be because of your evening with a certain baker?"

I gasp, and now it's my turn to stare back at them with wide eyes. "Uh, what? I didn't—"

Before I can start my denial tour, Ms. Flores cranes her neck and focuses her attention behind me.

She whistles. "Looking sharp, Mr. Sharpe."

Malcolm appears at my side in a gray, herringbone suit. I try to pull my eyes away as he adjusts his cuffs, but I can't.

"Wow, what's the occasion, Malcolm?" Sharlene asks.

"It's the big day with the distribution execs," Ms. Flores answers for him. She claps her hands together once and places them under her chin. One of the things that I've come to love in just a few short days is the way

Ms. Flores looks at Malcolm like his mother would. I get why he'd settle here in Holly Oaks. There are cracks in him that this town fills. It's the first time I give him the credit that maybe he *is* different.

Malcolm finishes fiddling with his cuffs "Yup. Been putting it off long enough."

Ms. Flores takes a sip of coffee. "I'll say. Thank God you got the ball rolling. Felt like you might have been waiting until next Christmas."

Malcolm laughs, and Ms. Flores glances at me over her coffee cup. I am certain that I'm gawking, but I can't stop staring up at him.

"Morning, everyone."

It's that greeting that finally gets me to take my eyes off Malcolm.

Otis enters our little group discussion. He takes off his thick beanie and hangs onto it with both hands as we all say good morning back to him.

"Everything okay?" Ms. Flores asks, her brows already furrowing.

Otis smiles. "Everything's fine. Just wanted to give you an update, actually. We won't know if things are working for a bit, but the process is going well. Things seem to be running smoothly."

"That's good news," Malcolm says.

Otis nods. "We're about twenty-five percent, though.

Don't quote me, but I think things are gonna be okay."

"Good thing we had a secret weapon," Ms. Flores says.

"The plant food is the best on the market," I say.

"I was talking about you." Ms. Flores winks at me.

"Agreed," Malcolm says.

Otis puts his hat back on his head and adjusts it. "Extremely lucky. I've got to get going. We still have more ground to cover."

"Thanks, Otis," Ms. Flores says.

He gives a slight bow. "I'll see you all later. I'll be out on the west side for most of today. Call me if you need anything." And then he's gone.

My eyes can't help themselves and find their way back to Malcolm. I notice his tie is a little crooked, so I stand. He's not quite expecting me to, though, and he turns at the same time, the two of us bumping into each other. He extends his hand to steady me at my waist, and I need it because something thunders through me, another chemical explosion from him being so close. When I give a quick nod that we have an audience, his hands drop immediately.

I smile up at him and fight my urge to lose myself in those eyes. "Your tie." I place a hand on the bottom and then one at the top and straighten it. "It was a little crooked."

"Thanks," he says, looking at the floor then back to me. "I was never good at tying these things."

"You've come a long way," I say.

He rubs the back of his neck. "Not bad for a small-town guy, huh?"

I nod. "Go get 'em."

He grins.

"You got this, Malcolm," Sharlene says.

Ms. Flores points to Sharlene. "What she said."

There's one more burst of laughter before he tells us goodbye and disappears.

When I turn around, Sharlene and Ms. Flores are studying me.

"What?" I ask, reclaiming my seat.

Sharlene brings her mug to her lips and shrugs. "Nothing. Nothing at all."

I know her well enough to know it's absolutely something. I roll my eyes at her.

Ms. Flores stands and reaches for the coat and scarf hanging on the back of her chair. "I could use some fresh air. Rose, do you want to take a walk with me?"

"Of course," I say.

She links her arm in mine. It's an innocent gesture, but it makes me wonder what she's up to.

As Ms. Flores and I stroll around the Holly Oaks property,

I find myself not hating the crisp air as much as I did when I first got here. That confuses me, though. How can weather I'm not used to grow on me in just a few short days? And it's not just the weather. There are other things that have grown on me too.

Ms. Flores breaks the silence lingering between us. "Something on your mind?"

I stick my hands in my pockets. "Just wondering how I came to liking this weather."

She chuckles. "This place will do that to you. And how can you look at these trees and not fall in love with them? I'll forever believe in their magic."

I nod. "It's been great spending time with them...and everyone."

"We've loved having you here. I know Malcolm is really glad to have you around." She cuts me a quick look then refocuses her attention to the distance in front of her.

"Me too. Even if I wasn't thrilled about it at first." I laugh, remembering all my protesting. Parts of me still want to protest. But the truth is, Holly Oaks really has worked its magic on me. I feel...different.

Ms. Flores pats my arm. "I wish you could stay longer. We sure could use someone like you around these parts."

I scrunch my face. "But what about the sale? The whole point of me helping to figure out the tree situation was so you could ensure the sale of the tree farm."

She offers a faint smile. "You know, Rose, when you get to be my age, you become a good judge of character. I haven't met a buyer yet that would make me one hundred percent confident they'd do right by the tree farm. But I've been thinking a lot lately that maybe the sale needs to be an inside job." She clutches my arm tighter.

I stop walking. "Wait. So what are you saying?"

She squares her shoulders and faces me. "I'm saying you have the skill set and, most importantly, the heart to run this place."

Somewhere in the distance, a Christmas record scratches—or maybe it's just in my head. I can't tell, because clearly I can't tell fantasy and reality apart. Did this lady really say she thinks I, Rose Douglas, am the best person to run a Christmas tree farm? And not just a Christmas tree farm. A Christmas tree farm *and* lodge.

I take a deep breath and release it, watch it waft in the cold air. "Ms. Flores, as flattered as I am, I can't buy a tree farm. I don't have that kind of money. And the maintenance...I'd have no idea what I'm doing."

She lifts an eyebrow in mischief. "Which is why I have a proposition."

I blink. "Okay..."

"What if you stuck around? I could pay you a salary or consulting fee—whatever you want to call it. I'd show you the ropes, and eventually, you could take the reins."

"You still haven't addressed the money—that I don't have." It's ludicrous. Imagine me, running an entire tree farm and lodge. It's the last thing I'd ever have on a bingo card with my name at the top of it. Part of me is flattered, but the larger part screams, *no way*.

"We can figure something out." She's so cool about it, like we're discussing what to have for dinner later this week.

I stare into the distance at the snowy trees and mountains.

"Ms. Flores...I—"

She waves an arm in the air. "You don't have to make a decision right now. I know you've been working on growing your own business. Plant Ladies, right?"

I nod.

"I know you can't just walk away from that. I'm just putting this out there. Giving you an option in case you want to take a risk. Might be worth it." She winks.

I bite my bottom lip, my head suddenly a tilt-a-whirl. "It's just a lot to unpack."

"Of course it is, dear." She pauses. "And not to give you another item to unpack, but there might be another risk that'll be worth it as well."

My eyes go wide when it dawns on me what she's referring to—or rather, who. "Ms. Flores."

She shrugs and offers me her signature sugar cookie smile. "I'm just making sure it's out there."

Twelve

I'm out of sorts for the rest of the day after my talk with Ms. Flores. So much so that Sharlene continuously asks me what's wrong. I analyze every possible outcome. What happens if I stay? What happens if I go? How does Plant Ladies fit into it all either way?

Like any logical person would do, I hop on my laptop at the kitchen table in our cabin the following day and scour the internet in search of new clients for Plant Ladies. *I'm going home at the end of this trip. I'm going home at the end of this trip.* I repeat it in my brain like it's my new mantra.

Sharlene leans over my shoulder. "That"—she points

at the screen—"does not look like R&R."

"That's because it's not."

Sharlene gives my shoulder a light push then moves so that she's at my front instead. She crosses her arms. "ROSE."

I copy and paste an email address to my contact list. "What? Look, I admit this trip has been a lot of fun. But we have to go back home, and we need new clients to go back to, or we won't have a business soon."

"You can worry about that later." She takes a seat. "And where is this coming from? I thought you were finally starting to have fun. But you've been acting weird since yesterday."

I shoot her my on-the-verge-of-a-meltdown look.

Her eyes drill into me, playfulness dissipating. "I know that look, Rose Douglas. What's going on?"

I sigh. "I had a conversation with Ms. Flores yesterday."

"Okay, that doesn't sound so bad."

"She offered me a job."

Sharlene is quiet for a few beats. "Okay, I'm going to need more details than that."

"Ms. Flores seems to think she can teach me to run this tree farm then take it over. Oh, and she'll figure out how to eventually sell it to me."

Sharlene blinks.

When she doesn't say anything, I say, "I know,

wild, right?"

She slaps her hand on the table, and my heart startles in my chest. "Are you kidding? This is the perfect opportunity for you. You could do a job like that with your eyes closed."

I shake my head. "I can't uproot my life, Sharlene."

"Why not?" She pushes her shoulders back like she's getting ready to battle me.

"Because I—" I stop there because I actually don't know.

"Exactly. There's nothing that's tying you permanently to Orlando. We're the bosses. We can operate Plant Ladies from anywhere if we had more help. *And* maybe you can see where things go with Malcolm."

I shoot her an irritated look. "First, slow down. Second, been there, done that. We're just friends." I'm about to explain further, but then my phone buzzes.

"That's him, isn't it?' Her voice gets higher at the end of the sentence.

I stare down at the text on my phone. "He wants to meet for dinner."

"Just as friends, though." Her voice is all sarcasm.

"It's because we need to talk about the trees and the next steps they'll need to take before I leave."

"Right. You're the only one who can't see what's in front of you."

"He's..." I pause as flashes of our relationship play out

on a movie reel in my mind. "He never said he wanted more. He's *never* said the word love, actually. And I can't keep risking him. If I do this again, it needs to be with someone who wants me in permanent marker."

Sharlene lets out a frustrated breath. "This trip is your chance to find your answers."

I stare back at her, because what else am I supposed to say?

"Don't just sit there staring at me. Answer the man, and ask him what time."

I type out a text asking if 7 PM is okay. Almost immediately, my phone buzzes back. When I open his text, I see the words, *it's a date*. I don't want it to make me smile, but I do. I also can't help thinking of Sharlene's words. What if I could use this trip to find out?

I decide to walk to Sugar Cakes so I can be alone with my thoughts. By the time I get there, I'm a glacial wreck. My hands are cold and clammy inside my gloves. My pulse pounds in my ears. My stomach ties knot after knot. Why am I nervous? This is just Malcolm. Malcolm who I've known forever. Malcolm who used to be my best friend. But maybe that's just it. Maybe I'm nervous because he isn't my same Malcolm. And I'm not exactly sure what that means or what it changes between us—maybe nothing.

I let out a deep breath as I stand in front of the bakery door. I already see the overhead lights aren't on. There's only a soft glow illuminating the inside. It does give me pause. I push the door, and it opens. The bells jingle.

I close it behind me and lock it. I've watched enough Lifetime movies to take any chances, despite the fact that everyone in Holly Oaks is comfortable with unlocked doors. To the left of me, in the corner of the bakery, is a table with a black linen tablecloth, two place settings, and candles. I take a few steps toward it. It's then I see it.

The doors to the kitchen swing open, and Malcolm slips through, holding a bottle of wine cradled in his arm. He stops when he sees me, and it's like our eyes are programmed for each other.

"Hi," I say first. It's the only thing I can get out, and I think that's because I know I'm supposed to say it. My brain refuses to form words otherwise.

"Hi," Malcolm says. And I wonder if his brain is doubling down too, refusing to make words.

It's a few beats before I snap myself out of the haze. "What is all of this?"

"For you," Malcolm says.

I unbutton my coat and start to take it off, but before it's down my arm, Malcolm is at my back, helping me slip it off. There he is, close again, ratcheting up all my nerve endings. He drapes it over the chair then pulls the chair out for me to sit. I do.

"I do have a question, though," I say.

"Shoot."

"Why all this for me?"

"Because you helped me out of my comfort zone. And because you helped with the tree farm. And honestly, for bringing joy to Holly Oaks. All this"—he gestures around—"isn't even enough."

I look away from his intense gaze, feeling my cheeks warm. "I didn't really do anything. I was only trying to help."

He pours water into the glasses on the table. "It's so much more than that. You're inspiring, Rose."

I fiddle with one of my loose curls, the heat continuing to spread under the skin of my cheeks.

Malcolm finishes pouring the water. "And because of you, it looks like I'll be taking the risk with the distributors."

I sit up straighter, clasp my hands together, then rest my chin on them. "I want to hear all about it."

"Before we do, I've got a surprise for you."

I tilt my head to the side. "I thought this was the surprise." I point to everything in the cozy romantic corner he's created.

"Not even close. I'm on a mission tonight."

He inches away from the table. "Be right back." While he's gone, I try to reason with my heart, tell it that we've been here before and maybe we should keep our emotions secured and in a safe place, but I'm not exactly winning the argument.

Malcolm comes back with a tray of various dishes. And it smells familiar and savory and sweet all at once. He sets the dishes down on the table then sets the tray on the counter where the cash wrap is. He uncovers one of the dishes.

I look at the dish, then back to him, and repeat the steps a few more times.

His smile widens like he's pleased with my reaction. "That's what I was hoping for. I know it's your favorite."

I stare at the dish of shrimp pelau. It had always been my comfort food. Gran used to make it for me growing up. I stopped eating meat when I was thirteen. Our family always used beef, but Gran thought shrimp would work just as well with the sweet coconut milk rice. It was the first dish she modified after my declaration.

"I, um..." I clear my throat. "I can't believe you made this for me."

"I remembered how much this dish comforted you and how much it meant."

I swallow and look at him, remembering why past Rose loved him. He's still in there.

He places a hand on the other dish cover. "One more surprise."

"There's more?" He's already done so much.

He uncovers the dish to reveal a square, delectable piece of white chocolate speckled with pink and a carved rose at its center. "I've been feeling a lot of inspiration lately, and we have a new permanent menu item. Meet our Rosettes. They have a hint of rose infused in them."

It's all so sweet but overwhelming as my emotions tangle and knot. I look up at him, my heart absolutely unhinged in my chest. "Thank you, Malcolm."

"You're welcome." He takes a seat. "You know, when you first got here, I'm sure it seemed like I was acting weird about you being in Holly Oaks. But I was just surprised. I'd been thinking about you lately, and then, there you were. And in my bakery."

My stomach flips. "You were thinking about me?"

He gives me a shy smile and takes a sip from his water glass. "Yeah. You're kind of a constant."

Butterflies, butterflies, butterflies.

I don't even know what to say other than that, so I switch gears. Malcolm starts scooping pelau onto my plate. "So tell me about how it went with the distributors. The suspense is killing me."

He laughs. "So they came prepared. They had this binder of plans, laying everything out for me to review.

It was intense, but I appreciated them going into such great detail. I was totally impressed. But then they said that they'd handle the entire distribution process. However, they do need initial training from me, which requires travel."

I nod. "And that's the part you're hesitant about because it would mean leaving Ms. Flores, right?"

He sighs. "Yeah. And they could tell that I was bothered by that. And then something happened that I wasn't expecting."

"Which was?"

"They said they had every intention of working with me. We can't get out of the travel, but they're willing to prioritize my schedule because they genuinely want what's best for Sugar Cakes since my success is also theirs."

I clap. "This is the best-case scenario. Are you going to take the deal?"

"I think so. They gave me a couple days to think about the offer. It would be a big risk, but it would also mean so many big things for Sugar Cakes."

I sit back and take him in, not caring that he notices. "I've always known that you were going to do great things. And now you are."

"Well, lucky for me, my muse found me just in time."

I smile and pick up my fork so I don't have to meet his eye.

"Seriously, Rose. I can't tell you what it's meant to have you here. I don't feel like I'm sleepwalking anymore. You inspired this move." He points to the dessert on the table. "And you inspired a new dessert. You're the most iconic woman I've ever met."

"You sure you have the right Rose Douglas? Half the time, I have no idea what I'm doing."

"That just proves my point further." He chuckles. "If you want to grow Plant Ladies, then go after it. But you're going to have to stop playing it safe. Some people are designed to stay in comfort zones—you are not one of them."

My chewing slows down as that thought lands. I have been playing it safe, haven't I? Even with Fern Gardens turning me down, it took me forever to get up the nerve to actually reach out to them. And if I think about before that, I haven't made any other major moves. I make lists of potential clients I want to reach out to, and then I don't actually contact them. It's just been a regular thing for me to put it off over and over. The reality hits me as I try to work out in my brain how I allowed myself to get away with this for so long.

"Sorry, I didn't mean to overstep..."

"No, you didn't. You're right. I've been living in my comfort zone." I swallow, my mouth suddenly dry.

He nods. "Just giving you something to think about.

I wanna see you win too."

I smile. "Thanks, Malcolm."

"Of course. Now, I'm so ready for you to try this dessert."

I laugh. "Are you sure you want to name a whole dessert after me?" Because the thing that's on a loop in my mind is, *this trip will end, and I'll be going home*. When he left Orlando all those years ago, I wanted to wipe every trace of him from the city. Would he really want a reminder of me all the time? We're under different circumstances now, but still.

"Of course I do. Look, I know you have to leave, but this way, you'll always be around. And in a way, I'll get to keep you."

And it's those words, *keep me*, that do me in. I feel it. Something else taking over. Does he mean those words the way I think he does? Because I want to keep him. I've always wanted to keep him. But after everything that happened with us, I'm scared to. And if I'm really honest, I don't know if it's possible to keep something I've never felt I really had.

Thirteen

harlene and I sit on a bench in the Holly Oaks Town Square, drinking gingerbread lattes after a walking tour that ended at the only museum in town. I stretch my legs out in front of me.

Sharlene cradles her coffee cup in both of her hands. "That was a fun tour. Who knew that the Flores family was only the third to ever own the tree farm."

I take a sip of my latte. "I know. It's understandable why it means so much to Ms. Flores."

We're quiet for a few beats, watching people weave in and out of stores, trying to get their Christmas shopping done.

"So how was your date with Malcolm?" Sharlene asks.

I shake my head. "It wasn't a date."

She rolls her eyes. "And Holly Oaks isn't the Christmas capital."

I roll my eyes right back at her. Then I sit up straighter and turn my body on the bench so I'm facing her. "It was nice. Actually kind of romantic...which also makes it all so confusing."

"Romantic?" Her eyes go bright like someone just plugged in the Christmas lights. "Okay, I need details."

"Yeah. He made my favorite dish and then made a mini dessert that he named after me." I fill her in on all the details and what Malcolm said. "It was really sweet, which kind of reminded me of the Malcolm I fell for."

Sharlene smacks my arm.

"Ow. What was that for?" I rub my now throbbing arm.

She sets her latte down on the seat between us. "ROSE. He. Made. You. A. Dessert. Named. After. You." She inserts a clap after every word. "I think it's safe to say he likes you. Or should I say, *still loves you*?" She picks her cup back up.

I look at the light dusting of snow covering the ground. "Love? I'm not sure Malcolm ever *truly* loved me."

"Oh, he loved you," Sharlene says, bringing her latte cup to her lips.

"I don't know about that."

She sighs. "He has feelings for you that run deeper

than this trip. I think you should give Ms. Flores's offer some serious consideration."

I cross my arms. "Come on. I already told you, I can't just—"

"Leave Orlando?" she finishes. "Now you know, as your sister, I'm gonna keep it real with you. I think you're making excuses because you're afraid of taking risks."

I shrug. "Maybe I am. But there are also a hundred other reasons why it can't work."

"And likewise, there are a million reasons why it *can* work. And there is one thing that's certain."

I raise an eyebrow. "Which is?"

"You'll never know if you don't try." She places a hand on my shoulder and squeezes. "I know you're scared to get your heart broken again, but sometimes, we need a second try to get it right."

I let out another deep breath.

"Promise me you'll give it serious thought." Sharlene drills her eyes into me.

I press my lips together and concede. "I will."

"That's the Christmas spirit." She laughs.

"You think you're so clever." I shake my head.

She keeps laughing, and when she's had her fun, says, "Now there's a sledding race I don't want to miss back at the main house in a few hours. You in?"

"Well, I've participated in just about every other

Christmas activity here. I've got nothing to lose at this point."

Sharlene smiles, and like the Chesire cat, it takes a few beats before it reaches her eyes. "My dear sister, I think you're finally catching on."

When we arrive to the main house, two women in suits are heading out the doors with Malcolm and Ms. Flores.

When I catch sight of Malcolm, I let my gaze linger before looking away, remembering there are other people around us.

Ms. Flores waves to us. "Oh, Rose, Sharlene. How was your sightseeing today?"

"Enlightening. We learned so much about Holly Oaks and the tree farm." Sharlene beams.

Ms. Flores gives her a knowing smile. "We were just about to give these folks a tour of the grounds." She gestures to the two women who give us pinched smiles. "These are the lovely women considering buying the farm—Kelly and Fallon."

Their pinched smiles hold the position, and this time, they both at least muster a hello.

"Want to come along?" Ms. Flores asks. She's posing a general question, but her eyes zero in on me.

Sharlene glances back and forth between Ms. Flores and me then says, "You know, I was really hoping to warm up by the fire and finish my latest read before the sledding contest. Why don't you go ahead, Rose?"

"Well, I—" Sharlene elbows me in the ribs to cut me off. I clench my jaw. She knows how much I hate that, but she's been doing it to me since we were kids. "Um, sure. I can tag along."

Malcolm smiles. "Great, I think we can all benefit from hearing more about your treatment plan for the trees."

The two women nod in agreement. I'm glad they're all in agreement, because my imposter syndrome would beg to differ.

Once we're out on the west side of the farm, I let the rest of the group take the lead and hang back. Malcolm notices then slows his pace until he's in stride with me.

"You okay?" he asks.

I try to smile, but I know it's faint. "Uh, yeah."

"I still know when something's wrong. What is it?" he presses.

"Well, first, I don't exactly know why I'm here. I'm just helping out as best as I can. I'm no expert. And two, I just don't feel great about those women. They're barely smiling."

He smirks. "Some would say you were the same when you arrived at Holly Oaks. Maybe they just need to warm up."

I smack his arm. "I'm serious. I'm just getting a weird vibe from them."

"Me too," he says.

Ms. Flores continues to lead the way, periodically stopping so the women can inspect the trees. At last, we complete our tour. I feel entirely out of place, so while everyone gathers in a circle, I keep my distance, sliding my hand under the branch of one of the trees to examine its needles. None of them fall off in my hand—a good sign.

I lean in and whisper, "You're doing just fine. You'll be all better in no time." I keep talking to them just like my gran would while keeping an ear to the conversation.

Kelly, the one with the dark French braid, speaks first. "I must say, the grounds overall are impressive.

Fallon, the platinum blonde, nods. "Agreed. Beautiful place."

Ms. Flores beams. "We take pride in what we do. We're also really lucky that Rose came to visit. She's been such a special caretaker for our trees."

I freeze mid-sentence when Fallon, along with everyone else, turns to me.

Fallon's Grinch smile stretches in the sunlight. "Is that so?"

Kelly's inky eyes narrow at me. "What exactly are you doing?"

"Talking to the trees," Malcolm interjects.

Fallon laughs. "Talking to the trees."

Kelly joins her in the laugh fest but falls silent when they notice Malcolm, Ms. Flores, and I are not laughing.

I straighten and square my shoulders. "Yes. Talking to them stimulates growth. There have been numerous studies. Plus, my grandmother had a flourishing garden, and her secret was talking to her plants every day." It infuriates me when people assume I'm ridiculous for this. I'd love to see them try to keep something green alive.

Kelly and Fallon look at each other, and for a few moments, there's an awkward silence lingering between us all.

Kelly clears her throat first. "Um, well, I'm sure there's something to it. We're planning to bring in the best experts to ensure the trees do well all year long and make the proper profit during the Christmas season."

Malcolm crosses his arms. Gosh, he's sexy when he gets serious. "But you all plan to keep the farm's natural beauty and the hometown feel, right?"

Fallon smiles, but it doesn't reach her eyes. My gut sinks. I understand what that kind of smile means ultimately.

"Sure. No need to worry about that. But we do have to boost profits to make sure we earn the return on investment. We will keep as much of the charm as possible while also acting in the best interests of our firm. You understand, right?" Fallon asks.

Malcolm hesitates then says, "Yeah..."

Kelly turns to Fallon. "I think we've seen all we needed to see here." She shifts her attention to Ms. Flores. "Shall we head back?"

Ms. Flores smiles, but her lips are pulled taut. "Yes, let's."

I look to Malcom. It reminds me of how we'd always talk to each other with our eyes. When I study his, it's clear what we're both thinking: selling to those two investors would be a grave mistake for Holly Oaks.

When we get back to the main house, the three of us stand in the lobby. Even though there's a cheerful holiday song playing in the background and people making memories with their loved ones nearby, we huddle together like shattered ornaments.

Malcolm places a hand on Ms. Flores's shoulder. "Ms. Flores, are you sure about these investors? Kinda get the feeling they're more focused on profit than people.

Sounds like they might consider getting rid of our traditions and more if it doesn't serve their bottom line."

Ms. Flores pats the hand resting on her shoulder. "It's not ideal. But profits are important, right?" She says this with absolutely no gutsy. She doesn't believe it herself. "Besides, what choice do I have? I'm struggling to keep up with things. And soon, you'll be even busier once you sign—"

Malcolm holds a hand up. "I'm not signing a thing if we can't find a satisfactory solution for you."

She cups a hand on his cheek. "You've been so good to me. But you have your own life to live."

"And I care about you and this farm. This is my home," Malcolm says.

Ms. Flores nods repeatedly. "I know. And we tried."

Meanwhile, I stand there as quiet as ever, trying to figure out the right thing to say.

Ms. Flores makes eye contact with me. "You've been awfully quiet, Rose. What do you think of the investors?"

I pause, taking my time to select my words. "I guess I don't exactly feel warm and fuzzy about them."

Ms. Flores sighs, and how I hate to disappoint her. Sharlene's words about taking the risk creep into my mind. It might be that alleged Christmas spirit or the magic from the trees that everyone claims exists, but something switches on inside of me. Somehow,

Holly Oaks has gotten under my skin, turned me into someone intoxicated with a love for holiday sweet bread bakeoffs, the piney scent of mountain air, gingerbread lattes, and arctic weather. How can I stand by and let it all be taken away?

"But you could hold onto the tree farm if you had someone to help you oversee the day-to-day operations and the health of the trees, right?" I ask. What am I doing?

Ms. Flores's lips turn down as she thinks. "Yeah. It's just too much for me now, and Malcolm is so busy. And we're such a small town. Everyone here has already settled into their pursuits—at least, at this moment, they have."

Malcolm scrunches his face then juts his chin at me. "Why, what's up?"

I fold my arms over my chest and pace. "And theoretically, if someone were to agree to taking on that job, you'd be there every step of the way to mentor them and make sure they could truly handle the job?"

"Of course," Ms. Flores says. She offers a hopeful smile. "Do you know anyone who might be willing to take the risk with us?"

My lips split to a grin, despite my attempt to control it. I chance a look at Malcolm, and he's not just smiling. He's looking at me the way I remember him looking at me right before he leaned in for a kiss. It catches me off guard, so I look away.

"I might—if the offer still stands?" I say. I almost can't believe the words when I say them out loud. But the truth is, Holly Oaks feels like home. It's a wild feeling, given my apprehension about setting foot in this town, but something here feels right. The trees, the farm, the people, the ridiculous love of all things Christmas. It's all magical and makes me think maybe that's what magic really is: people and place working in tandem to take hold of your heart.

"The offer is standing at skyscraper levels," Ms. Flores says, immediately pulling me in for a hug. "So you'll stay?" she asks.

Even though my stomach twists into knots, I say, "I'll stay."

I meet Malcolm's smoldering eyes again over Ms. Flores's shoulder. I try with everything I have to stop my heart from whirlwinding. But it's no use. It beats wildly to a tune that I'm pretty sure is just for Malcolm Sharpe.

Fourteen

I meet Sharlene, reading by the fire just as she said she'd be. In her hands is *Last Christmas Crush* by Mia Heinzelman, and in her lap is another novel called *Christmas in Full Bloom* by Denise N. Wheatley. She really is submersing herself in this Christmas culture. She looks up when she sees me and closes the book.

Her lips spread into a smile. "There she is. You've got a glow, and it's not from all the Christmas lights in here."

I plop down on one of the comfy chairs next to her. "I do not."

Her eyes glimmer against the fire light. "Yeah, you do. Now tell me, is it Malcolm, or is it that green thumb of yours?"

I side-eye her. "For the millionth time, I'm good on Malcolm." I pause, still not believing that I just agreed to a major life change. "But I did take the job."

Sharlene squeals. "Yes!" She throws her arms around me. "I'm so proud of you, sis."

"You are?" I ask.

When she pulls back, her eyes are glassy. "You have no idea how happy I am for you. I've watched you just bury yourself in work over the last few years. To be honest, I was getting a little worried. Life is about more than business and clients. And there is such a thing as being too cautious. I think Holly Oaks has been good for you. And now that I've seen you here with Malcolm, I think he might be good for you too."

I sink back in my chair and stare up at the ceiling as my brain and heart decide to spar with each other.

"What's wrong? Aren't you happy?"

"There's so much I'm worried about, sis."

"Like?"

"What about Plant Ladies?" I ask.

"We'll work it out. I can handle things in Orlando while you're here. And you can work remotely too. And each of us can travel back and forth as needed. I wouldn't mind an excuse for having to hop on a plane for a mountain getaway." She winks.

Of course my sister would use this as an opportunity

to travel. "Or maybe there's an added benefit shaped like a Ralph?"

We laugh.

"And who knows. Maybe that's something we can talk about. Maybe Plant Ladies needs to be reimagined. Maybe Orlando isn't the place we thrive in."

I sit up straight. "Wait, what?"

She holds up both hands. "We don't have to make any rash decisions. But I've had a great time here. Maybe we move our headquarters."

I swallow. "You'd move to Holly Oaks?"

She shrugs. "Why not? I'd miss our parents, but I've always hated the hot weather."

I smile. "Me too."

Sharlene rests an elbow on her armrest and places her chin in her palm. "Just one more thing to iron out."

I sigh again. "Malcolm has never been good at communicating his feelings. It didn't matter how much I loved him. He was always up and down. And he's still not clear now. Like, I can see myself falling again, Shar. And he does really sweet things and sometimes says them too. But I know that all too well. He's let me down before."

"He was a different person then—someone grieving, lost even. I think there were so many big emotions, and he just didn't know how to deal with all of them, let alone take on someone else's emotions. But now? When the two of you are in the same room, it bursts into flames. The risk is calling," she says.

I don't know how the thought gets in, but I think, *maybe I will.*

Behind the main house, there's a hill just beyond the clearing where the giant tree we lit up a few nights ago lives. As I now know to expect, most of the town is already gathered. Some people are practicing sledding down the hill with the only two sleds available, while others chat with a warm drink in hand. I have to admit, it feels a little like joy while I watch.

I catch sight of Mayor Gregory in her puffy coat and snow boots. She adjusts the cord on a microphone connected to a mini amplifier. She lifts the mic. "Welcome to the sledding games, everyone!"

The crowd claps and woots. "I hope you all brought your snow game!"

More cheers and an explosion of laughter.

"If you haven't already, please make sure you add your name to the drawing box. We'll randomly select two people to race against each other. Remember, this is just for fun."

A few people boo.

"See? That's exactly why it had to be said. Some of you are a bit too competitive." She chuckles.

Sharlene leans in and whispers, "I already added our names to the drawing box earlier today while you were out with the investors."

My stomach lurches. "What? I was just gonna watch. I have no desire to go sliding around in the snow." I could honestly kill her right now.

She shakes her head like my response simply won't do. "That's no fun. And we came here to have fun."

"Correction, *you* came here to have f—"

She nudges my arm. "Look, it's starting."

While we were having our disagreement, Mayor Gregory called the names of two people. She's now standing between both riders, holding a large flag with a Santa Claus carrying a bag of toys. The thing is almost as tall as she is.

"Now, remember, you must wait for me to wave the Christmas flag.

Both sledders nod.

Mayor Gregory makes a big show of holding the flag out and pausing. "On your mark." She looks back and forth between both sledders. "Get set." She lifts an eyebrow. "Go!" She waves the flag. The vibrant Christmas colors on it blur as it waves against the backdrop of a crisp, blue sky.

The two sledders take off with a running start, hopping into their sleds right before the drop down the hill as everyone screams and cheers for their respective person. I look around. There are only endless smiles, fun that feels tangible, and a new kind of warmth that fills me all the way to my toes. It's then I realize I'm falling under the spell of this town. Damn those trees.

All the cheers get louder as the sledders reach the bottom of the hill, and the winner throws both hands up in victory.

"Now for the next set of sledders." Mayor Gregory reaches into the box and pulls out two more slips of paper. "Racing against each other will be Malcolm Sharpe and Rose Douglas!"

Oh no. I am definitely going to kill Sharlene. This is all her fault. When I look at her, she claps once then jumps up and down. Meanwhile, my stomach flips. I hate when too much attention is on me.

I shake my head and start to say, "Maybe someone else should—" But Malcolm emerges, grabs my hand, and pulls me over to the sleds. I want to protest, but the contact suspends the words in my throat. I imagine them dead center and dangling. No way up, just left to die.

When we get to the sleds, he doesn't let go of my hand and, instead, leans in near my ear. "Time for round two. You might know how to make a good sweet bread, but this is my terrain. I know it like the back of my hand. Revenge will be mine."

I laugh and push my index finger into his chest. "Good luck with that, Sharpe. I'll be waiting for you at the finish line."

Only then does he let go of my hand, and we go to our respective sleds. I remember then that I saw on a TV show once that the secret to winning was getting a proper running start. I take my stance, ready to run. Around us, the crowd sounds rowdier. Or maybe that's just because I know all eyes are on us, and my nerves are reckless. Mayor Greogry takes her usual spot between the two of us.

"On your mark." Her voice booms over all of us.

My heart accelerates, and I feel my palms getting sweaty under my gloves, despite the cold.

"Get set..."

I steal a quick glance at Malcolm, who's looking at me with a wide smile. I try to fight a smile, but I can't, so I give in, snapping my head back to the path in front of me.

"Go!"

We run, jumping into our sleds at the top of the hill and picking up momentum the farther down we move. The wind whips through my curls, my adrenaline pumping as we zoom down the hillside. Malcolm reaches over to my sled and tries to push me off track. I gasp. He misses and tries again. I shriek, then laugh, managing to hold him off as we get more competitive. My determination to win isn't a match for him, though, and when we make it to the bottom, I come in just a second before he does.

Jumping to my feet and lifting my hands in the air, I shout, "I won!" It almost hurts to smile—my face stiff from the frigid air.

"Not a fair race," Malcolm shouts, returning my smile.

"Because you cheated," I say, placing my hands on my hips.

I don't even see it coming. A giant glob of something slushy shatters against my coat. When I look up, I see Malcolm laughing. I gasp, and just as I'm about to gather my own pile of snow to get him back, he takes off through the woods in the distance. I'm not letting him get away with his little snowball trick, so I chase after him. As I run, the frigid air whips against my face and into my lungs. So much so that I'm convinced my insides will be all frost when we finally stop. I will my legs to move faster. He starts to slow down, and I gain some distance. He stops and spins around to face me. Just as I almost reach him, I bend down, grab a handful of snow, and throw it at him. He tries to duck, but it catches the side of his face.

We both stop.

"Oops," I say sheepishly.

He smiles. "This means snow war," he shouts.

I run, and this time, he's the one on my heels. I make a mental note that I clearly need to do more cardio because I'm pretty winded. He closes in on me and at last reaches me. I start laughing as he wraps both his arms around me and scoops me up. The tall trees that surround us move in a blur as he twirls me around.

I squeal as I try to wriggle out of his grasp. It's then that I stop laughing because I'm suddenly hyperaware of how his strong hands grip my thighs. He finally sets me down, and when he does, we're chest to chest. There's nowhere to look but into his Milky Way eyes.

"Caught ya." He brushes the tiny bit of snow off my nose then reaches for one of my loose curls and twirls it around his fingers then tucks it behind my ear.

"I wanted you to." I suck in a breath when his index finger traces my jawline. *Butterflies, butterflies, butterflies.*

"You're beautiful," he says. He leans down until our lips are inches apart, and I tilt my head up to meet him. My brain tells me to stop this right now, but my heart pulses, blood in my veins rushing.

And then his velvet lips meet mine, sweeping, and urgent, and intensifying. He pulls me tighter to him, and I wrap both arms around his neck, my fingertips trailing up. I feel him shiver under my touch. He holds me tighter, adding more pressure. It's all familiar and new at the same time. Like an improved version of your favorite comfort item. It's the thing you return to again and again. The thing you can't get enough of. The thing you also don't want to end.

Except, it does, because my phone rings in my pocket, startling us apart. I jump back, push my hand in my pocket to take it out, then silence it. It's the same Orlando number that's been calling me. I stare at it for a few beats longer than necessary—anything to not have to address what just happened.

I look up at Malcolm finally, and he's looking at me like he wants round two.

I swallow. "Um, we should probably head back. Sharlene is probably looking for me."

He opens his mouth to say something, but I start trudging through the snow, pixelated heart and all.

Fifteen

After the longest awkward silence of my life, we get back to the main house where everyone is gathered to warm up after being out in the cold. I spot Sharlene chatting with Ralph near the fireplace. She looks up and waves us over when she spots us.

She takes a sip from the Santa Claus cup she's holding and smirks. "Where'd you two disappear to?"

Ralph's giving us an accusatory look too. "Yeah. Everyone was looking for you."

Malcolm and I look at each other for a second then look away. My heart thrums at the memory of our kiss in the woods. I haven't had a chance to process that, so I try

149

to push the images away, even though my lips still tingle.

Just as I'm wracking my brain trying to think of something to say, my phone rings. Everyone's attention shifts to me as I reach into my pocket. On the screen is that same Orlando number. This is just the thing I need to get out of the conversation.

"I should probably take this," I say, already backing away as three puzzled faces stare back at me. Better to have them confused than to think about how to answer Sharlene's question. I speedwalk to the door that leads to the back deck then press the answer button once it shuts behind me.

"Hello, this is Rose Douglas," I say.

"Rose, hi! It's Carmen from Fern Gardens."

I swallow, my mouth suddenly dry. What? "Uh, hi, Carmen."

"You are one difficult lady to get in touch with," Carmen says.

I let out a nervous laugh, wondering what she could possibly want after turning us down. "I actually left the city for a vacation with my sister. I haven't been really checking voicemails." I resist the urge to say I'm also here because of her rejection.

"That explains a lot. Are you far?" she asks.

"Yeah, actually. I'm in a place called Holly Oaks. It's in Colorado."

"I see. Well, rest up because we've got an offer for you. We just acquired a new property, and we're hoping Plant Ladies will come on board to help maintain the garden," she says.

I feel an anxiousness cycle through me. "Oh." It's all I can manage out.

There's a pause. Maybe she wasn't expecting just an oh. "It's a slightly smaller property, but I think it could really benefit from your touch. You interested?" she asks.

My mind is a collage of the last few days: the time with the trees, getting to know Ms. Flores, relearning what it's like to love Malcolm. "I—I don't even know what to say." Especially because it's so unexpected.

"Say yes," Carmen says on the other end. "I thought Plant Ladies would be perfect for this, even when we were considering you for Fern Gardens, but I needed to make sure the sale was going to go through."

I let out a deep breath. Why am I not ecstatic right now? It's exactly what I wanted before I got on a plane to Holly Oaks. But that's just it—I got on a plane to Holly Oaks. That one single action changed everything.

"Can I think about it?"

Carmen pauses for the second time. "Sure. You probably want to talk to your sister too. But try not to let it take too long. We'd like to get going right away. Although the offices are closed to the public, we'd love to start onboarding and discussing your plans for the gardens. Could you be here by the twenty-seventh?" She says this like it's normal.

"That's just two days after Christmas." Who even am I? Pre-Holly Oaks, Christmas consideration was not a thing. But this would mean leaving on Christmas Eve. We'd miss Ms. Flores's annual party and Christmas.

"Listen, I know it's a tight timeline, but we really want to get moving. The sale was already held up an extra month."

I pinch the bridge of my nose. "Okay. Let me see what I can do. I'll give you a call in a day or two."

I can hear a clap from her on the other end. "Wonderful, Rose. I hope Plant Ladies will come on board. We'd be honored to have you."

I turn around to lean against the rails of the deck. Through the glass door, I have a clear view of the spot I left Sharlene, Malcolm, and Ralph. I catch Malcolm's eye, and he grins, stirring my heart for the millionth time on this trip. I smile back, hoping my face doesn't give away all my wavering. "Thank you, Carmen," I say.

"Merry Christmas, Rose."

"Merry Christmas," I say. It was going to be a merry Christmas. But now, I'm not so sure.

If only this call had come in when we first arrived, things might have been different. I remember again how Gran always used to say that rejections were redirection. And wow, have I been redirected. I sit in the living room of our cabin, waiting for Sharlene to bring me hot chocolate. Last night when we got back to the cabin, I told her everything about the offer and the kiss with Malcolm in the woods.

She emerges from the kitchen with two Holly Oaks Tree Farm mugs and hands one to me.

As I reach for it, I ask, "Extra marshmallows?"

"My, my. From Christmas Curmudgeon to Miss Christmas, huh?" She sits on the other end of the couch.

I give her a weak smile. "Maybe this place has grown on me."

She squeezes my leg with her free hand. "I can see that. It's not a bad thing, sis."

I sigh. "What am I going to do?"

"I can't answer that for you. Only you know what's right for you. I'll support whatever you decide."

"Even if that means we can't stay for Christmas?"

"I got you no matter what." She pauses and takes a sip from her mug. "But I admit, I'd be a little disappointed if we missed Christmas here."

"Me too." I think of having to tell Ms. Flores. "Ms. Flores will be too."

"Someone else might be disappointed too," she says.

"Be real, Shar. I've been here before. Malcolm will make you fall in love with him, but he won't say *it*."

She sits up and turns her body so that it's fully facing me. "Hold on. Are you in love with Malcolm?"

"I've never *not* been in love with Malcolm," I say. There. Now I've said it out loud—actually, it's the first time I've admitted it to myself. I've been holding space for him even when I didn't really know I was. Took me getting on a plane and seeing him again for me to realize it.

Sharlene sets her mug down on the coffee table. "I knew it. I could feel it the second you two saw each other at the bakery. You have to tell him."

I scoff. "And risk being the fool again? No, thank you. If he has feelings for me, he needs to be clear. I'm not going to pour my heart out to him a second time only to have him change his mind when it all gets too real."

She folds her arms across her chest. "So what are you going to do?"

"I'm going to take the job. Plant Ladies should be the priority. As much as I love Holly Oaks, it wasn't part of the plan." It's not lost on me that I'll be leaving Ms. Flores in the lurch. But the truth is, I think I got caught up in too much fantasy and Christmas magic. There's no such thing. I forgot my practicality.

"Plans can change," Sharlene says gently.

"And sometimes they aren't meant to be."

Sharlene presses her lips together while she thinks. "Well, he should at least hear it from you."

"I know." And I hate it.

Sixteen

harlene and I spend the next day upholstering our hearts with as much of Holly Oaks as we can. It makes me sad, especially because I decided that after we had our fix, I'd be breaking the news to Malcolm and then Ms. Flores.

It's around five o'clock when I show up at the front door to Sugar Cakes. My whole body feels like it's full of mud. When I peer through the glass, I see him and Ralph coming out of the swinging door, pastry boxes in each of their arms. They're laughing about something, and I think about how I'm going to ruin that mood with my confession.

I knock on the door, and Malcolm's smile when he

sees me makes me feel even worse. He hurries over and unlocks the door.

"Hey, Rose," Ralph shouts from behind the counter.

I wave at him. "Hi, Ralph." My voice sounds like it's been hosed down, despite my effort for the opposite. I fix my attention on Malcolm. "Can we talk?"

His smile fades. "Uh, yeah. Wanna go for a walk?"

I nod.

He tosses his apron on a table near the door then looks back at Ralph. "Be back in a few."

We start our walk in the town square, and we're quiet for a minute while I summon my will to tell him I'm leaving.

I clear my throat. "Sorry if I interrupted."

He gives me a small smile. "You're my favorite interruption."

God. I didn't think things could get harder, but when he says things like that, it makes me doubt all my decisions—and not just my current ones. My past ones too. "I need to tell you something."

"Me too. About the other day when I chased you, and we—"

"No, not that," I blurt. It comes out a bit more frantic than I intend. I know because I notice him bristle then try to cover it up.

"Okay, then. What is it?"

"I got the client."

"Oh." He waits a few beats. "Do you mean the clients who passed initially before you decided to come here?" His voice is low, like he's afraid to ask it.

"Yeah, they've got another property." I fill him in on the details, trying not to fall apart at the way his face transforms. His smile slips and slips until it's nonexistent.

"This is really great, Rose. They'd be idiots not to work with you and Sharlene. I'm happy for you."

"Thanks," I say.

"So I guess this means you're not staying." He doesn't look at me when he asks it.

I bite my bottom lip. "It's just...I've been working for this for so long. They're my dream client."

He nods. "But what about Ms. Flores and m—" He stops himself and looks up at the sky.

"Ms. Flores and...?" I look at him now, but he keeps his head turned to the sky. I wait a few more seconds, hoping he'll say what I need him to.

"And the farm," he says.

That's what I thought. He still can't say it. He's exactly the same. I shake my head. I'm not sure why I allowed myself to hold onto any shred of hope that he might fight for me this time. "I don't love that. And I do hate to disappoint her, but you were the one that said I should take risks, right?"

"True. But sometimes a risk means jumping without the safety net below. Will that client be the safety net or a real risk?"

My blood boils. He has some nerve lecturing me about risks and safety nets when he's the one who can't even say what he feels. I fold my arms over my chest. "Would you say you're jumping without safety nets?" I challenge.

He swallows and stares into the distance like he's trying to work something out. "I'm just worried about Ms. Flores being devastated by this," he says.

He gets one more chance to say it. "Only Ms. Flores?"

But he just locks his jaw.

"Before you dish out advice about taking the right risks, you should make sure you're taking them yourself. I can't wait on you anymore, Malcolm." Everything inside of me cracks.

"Rose, wait," I hear him say to my back.

But I don't wait. I just keep walking, letting the distance between us expand.

After walking away from Malcolm, I paid a visit to Ms. Flores. The way her lips bowed in sorrow gutted me. I almost changed my mind for a third time. She was more than gracious, offering me a weak smile and pulling me in for a long hug then wishing me well.

I'm drained by the time I get back to the cabin, but I pack my things, take a shower, and slip into bed. I spend the night restless.

When it's time to get ready for our flight this morning, I feel like everything I do is in slow motion. Everything is heavy and hurts.

Sharlene and I have one more breakfast up at the main house. I try to savor it. Waking up every day and having a warm, cooked breakfast is something I'll miss—and lots of other things.

When our driver, Adam, arrives, we stand in the lobby, saying our goodbyes to Ms. Flores and Otis. No Malcolm in sight. I wish that didn't disappoint me.

I study Ms. Flores's worn eyes, and my heart breaks for a second time. "I'm sorry to disappoint you, Ms. Flores. I should have taken a bit more time to make such a big decision."

Sharlene nods in agreement. Even her unwavering excitement looks like it took a beating.

Ms. Flores, the gracious person she is, gives me a smile even warmer than the one she greeted us with on our first day here. "Don't worry about me, dear. I believe that things work out how they're meant to." There's a tiny glimmer in her eye, and before I can analyze that, she continues. "You need to follow that heart of yours, and that's what you're doing, right?"

Those words rip straight through the center of me. Of course I'm following my heart. I wanted this client. I have for a long time. "Yeah," I say. In my mind, those words were supposed to come out sure, confident. But instead, they come out faint and even a little shaky.

Otis places both hands on his hips. "Whatever client that landed you better recognize how lucky they are to work with you. I'm honestly a little jealous."

"Thank you, Otis," I say.

Another person I'm disappointing. Am I making the right decision?

He adjusts the beanie he's wearing. "Can we still call you if we need any advice on things here?"

"Of course." I smile, though I know it's not my best. "And although we won't be able to know until the treatment is complete, the trees seem to be stabilizing. Keep talking to them, okay?"

He nods. "I will. I'm a believer now."

"It's been the most wonderful time. I hope we can come back. Maybe we'll bring our parents next time," Sharlene says.

Something passes over Ms. Flores's face. Is she thinking what I'm thinking: will Holly Oaks still be here?

"We'd love that. Don't be a stranger," Ms. Flores says.

She pulls us both in for a hug and squeezes.

The door to the main house opens, and a gust of wind blows in. Along with it is Malcolm. Our eyes lock up, and I feel an ache so deep it's like being dragged underwater.

He swallows. "I saw Adam's car out front. Guess you two are heading out now?"

Sharlene nods her head yes. "It was good to see you again, Malcolm." She pats his shoulder. "I'll take our bags out to the car."

"I'll help!" Ms. Flores says.

"Um, me too," Otis chimes in.

And just like that, it's just Malcolm and me.

He sticks both his hands in his pockets. "I just wanted to come by and say goodbye...and wish you good luck—you know, with the new client and Plant Ladies."

"Yeah...thanks." I want to tell him more. How much I've fallen for Christmas and this town. And how it's all because of him. And how much I still want him even though he hurt me before. Even though he's still hurting me now. But what good would it do? I'm not enough for him, or he'd be straight with me.

"And I thought you'd want to know I signed the distribution deal. Took the risk."

"I'm happy for you." At least one risk is worth it.

"And I just want you to be happy, Rose."

I wish he'd understand that he could be part of that

equation. Happiness isn't just one thing. It's the sum of many things. I can make myself happy, but two things can be true. Malcolm makes me happy too.

I smile and try not to focus on my burning eyes. "Thank you for the best Christmas." I hold his gaze for as long as my tears will stay at bay. Somehow, this hurts worse than the first time we said goodbye. When I feel them ready to tip over the brim, I head for the door, and I don't look back.

Seventeen

There's a long, winding road lined with snow-covered trees that connects the Holly Oaks entrance to the lodging section. We're almost to the entrance when the car starts to slow.

"Oh boy," Adam says.

Sharlene and I sit up, the two of us leaning into the center of the backseat so we can see through the windshield. A giant tree stretches across the entire road.

"This can't be real," I say, sinking back into the seat.

Adam puts the car in park then opens his door. He steps out to get a better look, and I see him shaking his head. He pulls out his cell and makes a call, gesturing to the tree as if the person on the other line can see him.

Sharlene looks oddly calm.

"Why aren't you saying anything? Look at this." I point in front of us. "How are we going to make it to the airport in time for our flight?"

Sharlene just smiles. "Maybe the universe is trying to tell you something, sis." Her voice is soft and soothing. A stark contrast to the loud, erratic frequency of my heart.

I let out a deep breath and close my eyes. "All I want is to hurry up and get out of here before—"

"Before what?" Sharlene cuts in. "Before you lose your nerve to leave?"

I open my eyes and stare back at her, my stomach flip-flopping from being caught off guard.

Sharlene doesn't give me a chance to respond. "Because if you have to lose your nerve, that should tell you something. You're not sure. And honestly, as your sister, I know you. This isn't what you want. You're scared."

Adam slides into the driver's seat again. "Sorry, ladies. Looks like we're going to be delayed. They're not even sure they can get someone out here to work on clearing the road today."

"What?" I practically yelp.

"I'm sorry." Adam turns in his seat to look at us. "We can wait a bit if you want. Ms. Flores and Otis are making some calls. Or I can take us back to the main house. I'd understand if you wanted to wait and see first, though.

Up to you."

Sharlene opens her mouth, but I say, "Let's wait."

She sighs. "Let's say they can clear the tree. Are you absolutely sure this is the right decision? We haven't even left the property, and your emotions are a mess."

"I'm fine," I say flatly.

"Okay, we can wait a little," Adam says. Probably sensing we could use a moment, he takes a call coming through and steps out of the car again. I watch him pace in front of the car.

Sharlene places a hand on my arm. "It's okay if you're sad. You and Malcolm have all that history between you. I can feel disappointment radiating from you because he didn't say—"

"It's fine. I have a lot to be happy about. I'm going home to a new client that will give Plant Ladies momentum, I had an amazing trip with my sister, and I have a newfound appreciation for Christmas." No need to get too caught up on Malcolm.

Sharlene gasps. "So you admit it! You love Christmas."

"I said appreciation. Don't push it."

We both laugh, and it feels good to let some of the tension burn out.

She sits back, the leather seats squeaking under her. "I still think there was something rare and special with Malcolm. But you're gonna be okay, sis."

"As much as I love him, some things aren't meant to be."

She glances out the back window, her grin expanding.

"Why is that funny?" It's then I notice her eyes haven't left the back window. I turn to see what she's staring at, and my heart literally stops in my chest. My core tightens when I see a car door swing open, and *he* steps out.

Malcolm. He starts to jog toward us. When he reaches the car, he knocks on my window, slightly breathless.

I open the door and step out. "What are you doing here?"

He takes a deep breath. "Taking another risk."

"What risk could you possibly be taking when you've made it pretty clear where we stand?" I fold my arms over my chest. I don't mean it in a combative way, more as a way to protect myself.

He tilts his head to the side, studying me. "I don't think you understand."

"So make me understand."

"I walked away from you once, and I'm not going to let you go again."

There's a sting in my eyes, and my breath feels like it's stuck in my throat.

"You were right. I've been lecturing you this whole time about risks when I was too afraid to take them myself. When I left all those years ago, I felt wrecked. I thought that maybe if I had just been there, my mom's accident wouldn't have happened. And then I got it in my head that eventually you lose everyone. My dad lost himself, which led to me losing him. And that meant I'd lose you too. So I thought it would be best to just move on before I risked any of that. I was so broken and lost. I couldn't ask you to carry that too. You should have had someone whole, who could really see you. Not someone like me who couldn't see anything outside of the black hole he was in. But when you showed up here, I realized I'd been working this whole time to be the kind of man you deserved. And I think I am now, if this universe—you—might give me another chance."

My tears refuse to stay put. They slink down my cheeks, a contrasting warmth to the cold air.

Malcolm reaches for my hand. "And I've just been afraid of telling you because I thought that if I said it out loud, the universe would take you away from me, like my mom. But that's all wrong. I think the universe knows we belong together, and it's been conspiring this whole time to bring us to this point. You in Holly Oaks. Ms. Flores passing the baton of the farm, the trees, all of it."

"Take me away? I'm right here—I've always been." I reach for his cheek and hold my palm against it.

He presses his cheek into it, closes his eyes, and nods.

"I know. I have so much to tell you, but first I wanna tell you I'm sorry. I'm sorry for walking away then, when I loved you so much."

"I never wanted to stand in your way," I say quietly.

"I never thought you did. I've never been the best communicator," he says.

That gets me to crack a smile. "Ask me how I know?"

He laughs. "I've learned a thing or two over the last few years. And that's why I'm here. I would have chased that plane down the runway if I had to. I don't want to stand in your way either. But I hope you'll give me a chance to make this work. Whatever you want. If you want to go back to Orlando, I'll be your city slicker on every free weekend we have."

I laugh hard at that.

He brushes his thumb along my cheekbone. "I've always wanted you to be happy. But maybe you can be happy with me?"

"Yes," I say. "All I've ever wanted was you."

He tilts my head up and leans down, taking his time as his lips lower to mine. I wrap both my arms around his neck and press my body to his, all of me set alight. He breaks away first, pushing my curls back from my face.

"I love you," he says.

If I had to wait forever to hear it, it would have been worth it.

"I love you too," I say.

A car door flings open, and Sharlene runs around the back of the car to get to us. "Finally." She throws both her arms around us. "Imagine, I had to drag Rose hundreds of miles away from home and enlist the magic of trees to get you two to see the Christmas light."

"Magic of trees? Are you still on that?"

"I don't know, Rose. Ms. Flores swears by the magic of Holly Oaks," Malcolm says.

Sharlene points to the fallen tree still in front of us. "You think that was truly an accident?"

Christmas music. Laughing that resonates in my heart like multiple harmonies. Sweet bread. Glittery dresses and shiny cuff links. Warm lighting. Apples and cinnamon, and nutmeg, and chocolate. I take it all in at the Christmas Eve party in the main house. I almost missed this. I forgot how Christmas can make you feel. Warm and connected and full of hope.

Ms. Flores finds me. She looks adorable in her long, gold sequin dress and her cranberry lipstick. "Rose, you have no idea how happy I am that you're staying to help us out."

I smile at her. My heart hasn't stopped expanding

since Malcolm came to the car. "Me too."

"I'm so happy for you, sis," Sharlene says.

"So what will you tell the client in Orlando?"

"I actually spoke with them when we missed our flight. Sharlene is going to be there to oversee, and I'll be back and forth when needed or using video chat."

Ms. Flores raises the champagne glass in her hands. "That's wonderful, dear. I knew my trees wouldn't let me down. The best of both worlds."

I open my mouth to protest, but she just smiles sweetly and says, "Don't bother. Think of all the moments you had with Malcolm—the decorating, the field study, and now the thing that made sure Malcolm wasn't too late." She quirks an eyebrow.

Sharlene laughs, loving every bit of this show.

"I—" But I stop short because I really don't have an argument.

"That's what I thought." She winks. "Come on, Sharlene, Ralph just got here. Plus, you must try the cookies. We have twelve kinds for the twelve days of Christmas!"

They hurry off, giggling and whispering. I shake my head and make my way to Malcolm, who's standing by the tree. He reaches for me, pulling me close. There's a tingle on the spot where his fingers meet my hips. I wrap an arm around his neck and let the other rest against his chest, right where his heart is. The thing I love the most about him. The thing I always want to be close to.

"So I took one more risk," he says, his lips quirking up. "I called my dad."

"How'd it go?" I ask.

"We can't fix things overnight. We're going to start with a visit. He said he'd like to see the bakery."

I kiss his cheek. "I'm proud of you. I think your mom would like that."

He grins. "So tell me. How do you feel about Christmas magic now?"

Before I can answer, the lights on the tree next to us flicker. I stare at it, my mouth agape.

Malcolm laughs. "Told ya."

"Sometimes, when I spoke to them, if I really listened, I swore they were whispering back."

"And what did they say?"

"To take the risk."

I lift on the tips of my toes and kiss him, reveling in the thrill of having this every Christmas to infinity.

'Stay In Touch

I love hearing from my readers and seeing photos of them enjoying my books online! Tag me in your photos on

Instagram: (@racquelhenry)
Twitter: (@racquelhenry)
Facebook: (RacquelHenryAuthor)
TikTok: (@therealracquelhenry)

If you'd like to read a bonus scene with Rose and Malcolm, sign up for my newsletter! You'll also receive exclusive first looks, reading recommendations, access to subscriber-only giveaways, and all my writing news! Sign up here: racquelhenry.com/bonus.

:

Also By Racquel Henry

Juliet Washington left Orlando for LA five years ago to forget Ivan Underwood. When her company buys Ivan's magazine, she's forced back home to handle the transition—and what's worse, she must work closely with Ivan. Now more than ever she's determined not to let him get too close—he already broke her heart once.

After magazine editor, Ivan Underwood's boss informs him of a new parent company takeover, he never in a million years imagined the person handling the transition would be none other than Juliet Washington—the one that got away. At first, Ivan is looking for answers to the question that's been plaguing his mind forever:

Why did Juliet leave? But the more they interact, the more old feelings resurface, leaving Ivan even more puzzled. Does Juliet feel it too? For fans of Hallmark Christmas movies!

Note: This is a sweet romance novella, not a full-length novel.

Read *Holiday on Park*: racquelhenry.com/holiday-on-park/

After ten months of nursing a broken heart, Viola Evans is ready to move on—she just needs to let go once and for all. Determined not to let misery win, she resolves that she won't let anything get in the way of celebrating her favorite time of year: the holiday season. While participating in a Christmas activity one day with the children at her job, Viola writes a letter to Santa—surprising herself when she asks for someone new to make Christmas memories with. The question is, can she truly let go of the past and let love in again?

Charlie Palmer had to get out of New York City. After a confusing breakup with his ex, he makes a fresh start in Orlando. What he's not expecting to find is Viola Evans... or her letter to Santa detailing her deepest Christmas wishes. Drawn to Viola's charm and deep love for the holidays, Charlie finds himself wanting to give Viola the holiday memories she dreams of and Orlando starts feeling like home... that is until his ex resurfaces.

For Charlie and Viola, life has been complicated, but maybe all they need is a little holiday magic.

For fans of Hallmark Christmas movies!
Note: This is a novella, and not a full-length novel.
Read *Letter to Santa*: racquelhenry.com/lettertosanta/

RACQUEL HENRY

Love. Christmas. Second chances. Heartbreak. Greyson Reeves. These are the things Chanel Baldwin has quit. As far as she's concerned, Greyson Reeves is The Grinch Who Stole Romance—a.k.a. the guy that broke her heart. Since then, music's been her main squeeze, and she's become one of the most renowned flutists in the world, traveling the globe for performances. When Chanel finally makes it home for the holidays, her meddling mother asks her to help write a song for the neighboring towns' annual "Song of the Season" Contest. All Chanel wants to do is get the holidays over with, but she agrees to help—only to discover that the person she's helping is The Grinch himself, Greyson. She's not expecting her heart to drop the equivalent of ten stories when she sees Greyson—or that the more time they spend together writing songs, the harder it is to stick to that quit list.

One look at Chanel after so many years and Greyson Reeves is done for, never mind how many times he's talked himself into believing their epic love story was over. It was his fault things ended anyway. Chanel was going to travel the world as a principal flute with cream-of-the-crop orchestras, and he was going to do the same as a conductor. It would already be tough to make it work, and he wasn't about to stand in her way back then. Fate had not ruled in their favor. And it broke his heart too. But now? Let's just say working with her for the annual Song of the Seasons Contest isn't just creating a song on paper but in his heart.

What if the same person who splintered your heart is the same one piecing it back together?

For fans of Hallmark Christmas movies!
Note: This is a novella, and not a full-length novel.
Read *Christmas in Cardwick*: racquelhenry.com/christmas-in-cardwick/

RACQUEL HENRY

MEET ME IN
December

Giancarlo Westbrook isn't supposed to be home this Christmas.

To Felicity James, Giancarlo, a.k.a. her brother's best friend, is the unfinished draft that's never supposed to see the light of day. After one unforgettable kiss in college, which was strictly for educational purposes, they both agreed that memory should be tucked in a locked drawer. So what if they grew up sharing countless late-night dinners from The Golden Lobster, adventures, and whispered secrets under twinkling stars? The line in front of the friend zone is clearly drawn, and it's a line Felicity knows her brother, Clay, would hate for his best friend and sister to cross.

Six years later, they're both back in their hometown of Wedgefield for Christmas. Felicity, now an ornament maker, and Giancarlo, now a well-known muralist, are both at a crossroads in their careers. They're each looking for a distraction—and trying to ignore the spark that never went away—when Felicity uncovers an unexpected mystery from her grandmother's past. And she's determined to solve it. There's just one problem, Clay volunteers Giancarlo to help her. As Felicity and Giancarlo embark on a mission to solve the mystery in time to deliver the Christmas gift of a lifetime to her grandmother, they find themselves caught up in the familiarity and comfort of each other's presence. Maybe some drafts are meant to be finished. Maybe some stories need to be told.

Meet Me in December is a novella and NOT a full-length novel. It's a heartwarming romance very much like a Hallmark Christmas movie with no explicit scenes.

Read *Meet Me in December*: https://racquelhenry.com/december/

For Writers:

The Write Gym Workbook
The Writer's Atelier Little Book of Writing Affirmations

Racquel Henry is a Trinidadian writer, editor, and writing coach with an MFA from Fairleigh Dickinson University. She spent six years as an English Professor and currently owns the writing studio, Writer's Atelier, in Maitland, FL. In 2010, Racquel co-founded *Black Fox Literary Magazine* where she is Editor in Chief. Since 2013, Racquel has presented and moderated panels at writing conferences, residencies, and private writing groups across the US. She is the author of *Holiday on Park, Letter to Santa, Christmas in Cardwick*, and *The Writer's Atelier Little Book of Writing Affirmations*. Racquel's fiction, poetry, and nonfiction has appeared in *Lotus-Eater Magazine, Reaching Beyond the Saguaros: A Collaborative Prosimetric Travelogue* (Serving House Books, 2017), *We Can't Help it if We're From Florida* (Burrow Press, 2017), *Moko Caribbean Arts & Letters*, among others. When she's not writing, editing, or coaching writers, you can find her watching Hallmark Christmas movies.

Made in the USA
Columbia, SC
03 January 2025

48774223R00104